HILLS OF SILVER

WEST COUNTRY TRILOGY
BOOK TWO

HILLS OF SILVER

WEST COUNTRY TRILOGY
BOOK TWO

JOHANNA CRAVEN

ISBN: 978-0-9945364-7-1

CONTENTS

EMPTY LAND

He is afraid of her. She can tell.

Scarlett watches Asher as the carriage rattles and thuds.
They sit opposite each other on rough-hewn wooden
benches, crammed beside wool bales that smell of earth and
damp. He is forcing himself to keep his face impassive; jaw
tight, lips pressed into a narrow line. His eyes flicker to the
knife lying across her lap.

He could overpower her easily. She reaches his shoulder,
slim and slight. His muscular sailor's arms could break her
like a twig. But Asher Hales, Scarlett has come to realise, is
a coward. And as long as she sits with a knife in her lap, he
will follow her like a dog.

Once, she'd been drawn to this man. Had been drawn like
a lovesick heroine to the fall of his hair, the sharp line of his
jaw, his velvet voice and carefully chosen words. She had
been drawn to him back in those distant days when her

brother could do no wrong and her father's body lay on the sea floor.

Distant days.

They feel it. But it had been only that morning they had boarded the carriage in Polperro. Less than a day since Scarlett had seen behind Asher's velvet voice to the lies that lay beneath. Less than a day since he had produced his letter and everything Scarlett had known to be true had crumbled.

Her new world is harsh. Sharp-edged. She sees in bright colours, bolts of flame. Feels a chill in her chest and a simmering in the rest of her body. But she is glad the lies have been torn away.

Is glad to be seeing through clear eyes.

The carriage rattles, trundling from Polperro towards Portreath where, if the letter Asher has given her is to be believed, her father lives in hiding. The road snakes over balding hills and groves of trees blazing in the autumn. The sea has disappeared, leaving only the rise and fall of the land.

They have passed few others on the road. There is a strange emptiness to the place. An odd stillness between the bawl of the gulls and the rhythmic clatter of wheels through mud. Scarlett feels a deep pang of loneliness.

She shuffles uncomfortably as the carriage lurches. Her shift has bunched beneath her stays and she fidgets in annoyance. Everything is riling her; the shift, the smell of the wet wool, Asher's pathetic, doe-eyed cowardice.

She reaches into her cloak pocket and pulls out the letter. The page is thin and fragile. Sixteen years old.

She has read it so many times, she knows its contents from memory. But she reads it again, as though hoping she might find some hidden meaning, some new scrap of information.

Jacob is no longer in Talland, it says. *He left this place in his fishing boat, the village believing him drowned. On your return to England, you will find him in Portreath...*

Nothing new. Just the same, neat allegations. The father she had idolised had abandoned his children. Gifted them his unpayable debt.

Asher's eyes have shifted from the knife to the discoloured paper in her hand. His cheeks are flushed, the rest of his face ashen as though sickness had fallen over him the moment his dashing persona had been torn away. How can a man manage to be both flushed and pale at the same time, Scarlett wonders distantly? She shakes the letter at him.

"Who gave you this?" she asks again. "Who wrote it?"

Always the same response: "No one you know."

"But you trust this letter. You believe we will find my father in Portreath." Her words are thin as she voices the possibility. If she is to find her father, there will be no great reunion. She will not fly into his arms and lose herself in a flood of happy tears. No, if she finds her father, she will make sure he knows how she and her brother have suffered. The wild anger will rise inside her and she will not do a thing to stop it.

Asher nods slowly. "I trust the letter. Yes." He looks again at the knife. A sign he is lying? Or just a twitch of his nerves?

Scarlett grits her teeth in frustration. Asher Hales is both a liar and a coward. But he is also an intelligent man. A man that plots, plans, manipulates. A man who knows, surely, that keeping his knowledge close to his chest is the way to ensure his survival.

LOYALTY

The plan is sound. Forty ankers of brandy bought by a new agent in Saint Peter Port. Reuben's lugger to collect the shipment in. The Polperro caves in which to hide it.

A small venture, but Isaac hopes it will be a profitable one.

A secret one.

He and his crew hover by the fire at the Mariner's Arms. The tavern is closed to customers, but Flora has left the doors unlocked so they might plan their ventures away from the eyes and ears of Charles Reuben.

The conditions of the debt left to him by his father state Isaac must hand over his earnings to Reuben. And for fourteen years he has done just that; captained a smuggling lugger on an endless zigzag across the Channel, completing the runs and filling Reuben's pockets. Meanwhile, his family languishes in a world of patched clothing and sparrow pie.

He will do it no longer. He has spent far too many years paying for his father's mistakes.

On his last visit to Guernsey, he had met with an agent starting out in the business. A man willing to accept his meagre investment. The money made from this secretive run will buy passage for his family out of Cornwall. North, he thinks. Ireland, Scotland. Anywhere the past can fade, and Reuben cannot find them.

Will he earn enough from the sales of a single run? He can't be sure. He'll need enough for the journey and a roof over their head when they arrive. Enough to live on while he finds work. Enough for five tickets.

Four tickets, perhaps.

Isaac can't think of his sister without his anger blazing. He and Scarlett had parted that morning without speaking. Her last words to him had been ones of accusation, anger. Distrust.

He had given up his freedom to raise his sister. Shackled himself to Talland by plucking her from the children's home. And she repays him with distrust?

She can stay away, he tells himself. He has no desire to see her. And yet, the thought of her charging wildly through an unknown world makes something turn over in his stomach.

He pushes the thoughts of Scarlett aside. She is a grown woman now. Capable of making her own way in the world. He has his own business to attend to. Whether or not she will leave Talland with them is a problem for another day.

He tosses another log onto the fire, sending sparks flying up the chimney. Shadows move inside the empty tavern.

The crew are full of questions.

When? As soon as possible.

How? With Reuben's lugger.

Dangerous?

Reuben has sent gun-wielding men after him in the past. If he's caught making a run of his own, Isaac is sure shots will be fired.

But to the men, he says: "Thirty percent of the profits divided among you. Tell me you'll get figures like that from Reuben."

He's told just two of his crewmates of the voyage. All he needs to sail and load the lugger. John Baker and Will Francis are young men, good sailors. Trustworthy.

"How do you plan to leave the harbour without being seen?" Baker speaks in a whisper, as though afraid his words might carry up the chimney and drift across the village.

"We'll set sail in the night. Arrive in Guernsey by late morning. Store the goods in the Polperro cave when we return. I'll spread word before we leave that I'm taking the ship for careening."

Isaac catches a glance between the two men. His crew are in the trade for wealth. Smuggling can provide a life of polished boots and fine wine that farmers and miners can only dream of. A cut of thirty percent will have their attention. These men are loyal enough not to spread his secrets, yes. But he does not know whether their loyalty extends far enough for them to risk antagonising Charles Reuben.

"Thirty percent among us, you say?" Baker asks, calculating.

"Ayes. Thirty percent."

Baker holds out a hand. Isaac shakes, giving him a ghost of a smile. After a moment, Will follows. And loyalty, Isaac realises, can be bought by any man willing to pay the right price.

Caroline pushes back the curtain. Watches a line of silver smoke rise from a chimney of the Mariner's Arms.

She pictures her husband by the hearth, telling the crew of his plans in that gravelly half-whisper he uses when he has secrets to share.

She lets the curtain fall. She needs a yes from the crew. Isaac needs a yes. He has spent far too long as a slave to Charles Reuben, scratching at the debt of a father he had cared little for.

A debt, Caroline had said in the bliss of young love, that mattered little to her. She hadn't wanted to be that woman who thought only of silks and laces. That woman who turned away from a good man because of his empty pockets.

But twelve years of debt-ridden marriage have worn her down. Her love is no longer young, but their pockets are still empty. Her skirts are zigzagged with mending, boots patched so many times the soles are almost entirely made of pitch. Her son and daughter wear clothes outgrown by the village's other children.

Mary's smock gathers dust as she crawls across a floor that needs sweeping. She is bright-eyed and chatty. Caroline swings her onto her hip, pulling her smock down over soft pink knees.

"Well," she tells her, "if you'll not sleep, you'll come with me to see what's become of your aunt."

Mary fixes her with dark, knowing eyes.

Caroline pushes open the door of Scarlett's tiny bedroom. Her narrow sleeping pallet lies against one wall, blankets tossed messily across it. A candleholder sits beside the bed, clutching a cold, waxy stump. A stained apron hangs on the back of the door. The storage chest is open.

Caroline looks at the trunk, then at the baby. "Empty, of course," she says. "Are you surprised?"

Mary grabs at her mother's neckerchief. Caroline swings closed the lid and shoves the trunk against the wall.

So Scarlett has left. Flown from their lives in yet another dramatic statement.

Scarlett had been nine years old when Caroline had married Isaac. The day after their wedding, she had run across the cliffs and hidden in the cave at Polperro; a protest against the woman who had dared invade her home. The woman who had dared invade the life for two she had Isaac had built after the deaths of their parents. They had spent the morning searching before Caroline had convinced Isaac his sister would return when she felt she had made her point. Scarlett had slunk home as the sun began to set and gulped down two bowls of Caroline's onion soup.

Twelve years later, Scarlett is still self-centred and impulsive. No doubt she'll return to the house in a similar way soon, tired, hungry and craving attention. Point made.

Strong willed, Isaac has always said. *A difficult life.* Caroline is tired of him making excuses for his sister. Tired of him blaming Scarlett's behaviour on her upbringing, as though every word she speaks out of place lies firmly on his shoulders.

She pulls the blanket from Scarlett's sleeping pallet and tosses it onto her own bed. The nights are growing colder. No sense it lying unused.

There is no sign of Asher Hales, either.

Caroline snorts. He'd been plain old Matthew Fielding when she had known him. A new name for a new man?

Hardly. He'd been as deceitful and manipulative when Scarlett had brought him home as he'd been the last time Caroline had seen him.

The thought of those days brings tension to her shoulders.

She has stopped talking to Mary, she realises. Can't voice this dark chunk of her past, even to non-comprehending ears. Can't hear the reality of it spoken, or have the words hang in the air. What if her daughter should somehow absorb them and know the truth of who her mother is?

This part of her life must stay locked away.

Has Scarlett left with Hales? The little fool. Has she been blinded by his good looks and honeyed words? Just as she herself had been so many years ago, Caroline thinks wryly.

She lays the baby in the cradle. Rocks it until Mary's eyes are heavy and her own thoughts have begun to still.

Asher Hales has left. She can begin to breathe.

The door clicks.

Isaac is buoyed. His lips are upturned, hands in his pockets, the way they always are when he has news to share. As though the surprise of it is hidden in his fist. He tosses dark hair from his eyes and throws her a smile.

The men have agreed to the run, Caroline can tell. They are a precious step closer to that life without midnight landings and lantern-lit trading runs. A step closer to that life without Tom Leach and his rival smuggling gang, that life of avoiding revenue men in the street. A precious step closer to that life without Charles Reuben.

She'll not bring Isaac down by telling him about Scarlett's empty trunk. She knows how it will play out. His smile will disappear, and his hands will come empty from his pockets. He will drop everything as he always does and run into the night chasing his ungrateful sister.

No. Let tonight be about looking to the future. Let Scarlett find her own way home.

"The men will come?" she asks, joining him by the hearth.

He catches hold of her fingers and tugs her towards him. His hands are rough in hers. "Ayes. They'll come for thirty percent."

"And you've a landing party?"

"I will. A small one. Only the most trustworthy of the men." He plants a kiss in her plaited hair. "We'll be out of this place soon. I swear it."

She clutches a fistful of his coat. She wants him nearer. His hands in hers and kisses in her hair have become so unfamiliar. Their marriage has become a thing of one-word responses and terse *goodnight*s. Of silent suppers and love worn thin by the pressure of their debts.

Caroline inhales deeply, taking in his familiar smell of ash soap and sea. Things will be different once Talland is behind them. She is sure of it. Once Talland is behind them, they will start again. Everything breaking them down will fall away.

But she sees the unrest behind his eyes. How well she knows that worry he is forever unable to still.

"Any sign of Scarlett?" he asks, sliding his hands from hers.

Caroline sighs inwardly. "She's angry. Probably drinking herself stupid in Polperro. She'll come home when she's ready."

"I ought to go after her."

"No."

His eyebrows shoot up at her sharpness. Caroline looks away. She regrets shattering the peace. "She's a grown woman, Isaac. Leave her."

"And if it were one of our children run off into the night? Would you tell me to leave things then?"

"She isn't one of our children. Our children are here, caught up in free trade. We need to get them out of this life. Have you forgotten the things Scarlett said to you? She accused you of leaving a man to die!" Caroline hears her own bitterness. It is not animosity she feels for Scarlett, not really. Over twelve years she has managed a reluctant, obligatory kind of love for the girl she had had little choice but to mother. She wishes her no ill-luck, of course. But Isaac's mind is firmly on escape now. She will not let him be distracted by Scarlett's recklessness.

"I've not forgotten," he says, sliding off his coat.

He is staying. A small victory. Caroline touches his arm, trying for a gesture of solidarity. But he pulls away and carries his coat into the bedroom, reminding her that the wall they have built between each other is still as tall as ever.

THE LOST

The coach deposits Asher and Scarlett in Truro. Night has fallen emphatically; shadows lying thick and unyielding over the street. Water drips from awnings, plinking into the mud. The cloud bank is silver where the moon tries to push through.

Scarlett tugs her cloak around her. "How much further to Portreath?" She looks up the road. Down the road. Not at Asher.

"Several hours at least," he says. "We'll not find transport tonight. Best we look for somewhere to sleep."

She eyes him distrustfully. Does she have any idea of the path they are taking, he wonders? Is there any map in her head? Or does her knowledge of the world consist of her tiny village and that strip of sea between the Channel Islands? Her optimism may have capsized, but her naivety is still intact.

"How much coin do we have?" he asks.

She opens the pouch and lets Asher peer inside.

"Enough for a bed each," he says. He begins to walk towards the cluster of lights at the end of the street. Mud slides beneath his boots. He hears a dog bark in a distant alley.

Scarlett hurries after him. The knife is back in her hand, Asher notices uncomfortably.

"Where are you going?" she demands.

"I'm going to find us somewhere to stay. That's what you want, isn't it?"

She nods uncertainly.

"Put the knife away. No one will give us a room if they see you waving that about."

He waits by the door of the inn as she slides the blade back into her garter. She follows him to the counter.

"Two cheap beds," says Asher. He feels the sting of the words. His thirtieth birthday is far behind him and still his life is one of *two cheap beds*.

"We've beds in the back," the woman tells him. "Men beside the kitchen and women down the hall."

Asher nods faintly and reaches into the money pouch.

"No," says Scarlett. "That won't do." Her fingers dig into Asher's arm, silencing him before he can speak. "One bed," she says. "And a private room."

The woman behind the counter presses her lips into a thin white line. Scarlett cuts her with hard eyes.

"One bed," the woman repeats. "Private room. A shilling a night."

Scarlett jabs Asher's arm again and he hands over the money. The woman takes a candle from beneath the counter and lights it from the lamp. She hands it to Scarlett. "Let it blow out and it'll cost you a copper for relighting."

She takes the candle wordlessly, cupping a hand around the flame.

The woman hands Asher a key. "Top floor. First door on the left."

He nods his thanks and trudges up the staircase, Scarlett close behind. "What are you playing at?" He is grateful for the woman's threat over the candle. Scarlett's preoccupation with keeping it burning has silenced her for a time. He slides the key into the lock. The room is bare, with chipped white walls and floorboards indented by a century of footsteps. A lone bed sits in the centre of the room; a washstand and side table crammed into the corner.

Scarlett sets the candle on the table and looks at Asher. "I'm sure if I were to leave you to the men's quarters you'd not be there in the morning." She drops her pack on the bed and flings a ratty bolster at him. "You'll take the floor."

She slides off her cloak and empties the water jug into the bowl on the washstand. She leans over the basin, splashes her face. Back to him, she pauses, letting water roll off her cheeks.

Asher watches.

She is a loaded pistol with a knife in her garter. The darkness in her has taken prominence. Largely his own doing, he knows. He had used her, lied to her. Worst of all, he had been the one to break the news to her that her heroic, dead father is neither of those things.

Yes, there is guilt. Asher has enough humanity left inside him to feel a little remorse. He finds himself missing sunny Scarlett. Her optimism and blind trust had been a light among the bitterness of his life.

How much is this black-eyed terror capable of? Her life has been shaken at its foundations. She has lost faith in her brother, her father. Lost faith in Asher himself. He is sure the shock of it is enough for her to take that knife from her garter and spill a man's blood. He fears the blood will be his own.

Tread carefully.

Beneath the ice, there must be a little of warm, trusting Scarlett Bailey who had risked her life to save him from a sinking ship.

How long ago? It feels like a lifetime, but can be little more than a fortnight. Two weeks that have left Asher's life upturned. Left him directionless. Hopeless.

For more than a decade, he has dreamt of finding the hidden wealth of Henry Avery. Wealth that would see him educated to become the surgeon he has always longed to be. What a cold irony that it is here in myth-drenched Cornwall he has come to realise the haul is nothing but fantasy.

Scarlett turns back from the washstand. Her eyes are large and mournful like a deer's. She is as lost and lonely as he is.

"You must be hungry," he says throatily. "We ought to eat."

They sit at a table in the corner of the tavern. The only other people in the inn are a young couple in matching blue cloaks and an old man sitting alone at the bar. A fire hisses and spits in the grate, smoke spluttering up a chimney in desperate need of sweeping.

In spite of his unease, Asher is hungry. When dishes of watery stew come to their table, he eats in large mouthfuls. Scarlett stirs her supper in disinterest.

The food settles him a little. Brings a scrap of clarity.

So, the haul he has spent half his life dreaming of is a myth. He has no means of making a living, let alone earning enough for the university degree that would see him soar up society's ranks.

Scarlett has dragged him on a mission to seek out the man he has spent the last decade longing to come face-to-face with. Yet now, with the knowledge that Avery's haul is a fantasy, the thought of meeting Jacob Bailey again makes something turn in his stomach.

The reality of all this is miserable, but there is something vaguely steadying about taking stock of his life this way.

Look harder. There must be more.

Yes. He has a great mind. A great intelligence.

He must find a new way forward.

He needs another way to make money. And right now, the best option he has is to turn Isaac and Scarlett Bailey over to the revenue men. Lead customs to the heart of the Talland smuggling ring and collect a sizeable reward.

An impossibility, of course, while he's stranded here halfway to Portreath. He needs to get back to the south coast. Scarlett will sleep deeply tonight, he is sure. He will take her coin pouch, her knife. Find transport back to Polperro and the waiting revenue men.

He tries not to think of who else he will find when he slides back into the village.

Caroline had been in his thoughts almost constantly in the years he had been away from England. Each day he would find a different memory of her; coyly sipping brandy, teasing him with a hitch of her skirts, working his sharp mind with strings of probing questions.

She had been a shrewd seventeen-year-old when they had first met. He, less than three years older. They'd both been lodging in the creaking rooms above the Three Pilchards in Polperro. He had followed a trail of paltry fishing jobs to Cornwall and become entangled in free trade. Entangled in a world of tarred coats and fishwives. He had not expected to find a sharp-witted girl from London hiding among them.

He had fallen in love hard and fast. The life of greatness he imagined for himself suddenly had a woman in it. He saw himself in a lecture theatre, scrawling feverishly. Saw himself in the coffee houses, debating the merits of animism, convincing doubting minds of the soul's power over the human body. He saw himself performing dissections as an overflowing theatre held their breath. And he saw himself leaving the Barber Surgeon's Hall for a great Fitzrovia mansion. Saw Caroline there in rose-coloured silk and satin that sighed when she walked.

It was a perfect life that awaited him, once that money was in his hands.

His perfect life had not included conviction for assault, of course. It had not included indentured servitude in New England, or a decade of exile.

Each day of his sentence, he had dreamt of returning to her. But with each passing week, month, year, it seemed more and more impossible. Somehow, he would resurrect his life, yes, but he began to doubt that Caroline would be a part of it. Though he had tried to convince himself otherwise, he has always known her love for him had been tentative. A part of him knew she would not wait. There would be no new memories to replace the ones worn thin by time. She would be that shrewd girl of seventeen to him forever.

But then, there she was, crammed into that creaking cottage, Isaac Bailey's children dangling from her and the light gone from her eyes.

Asher couldn't make sense of it. How, after all that had happened, had she ended up in Talland as Isaac's wife?

She had known him at once. He had seen the blaze of recognition in her eyes the moment Scarlett had led him into the cottage.

He'd said not a thing to her, of course. How could he with Isaac or Scarlett or some snotty nosed child lurking around every corner?

Even if he could have managed a word, Asher could tell Caroline had closed down. She refused to look at him. Left the room whenever he was about.

He understood, of course. What a reminder he must have been. A reminder of her most regrettable deeds. Her darkest secrets.

How much would have fallen if Asher had opened his mouth?

Scarlett forces down a miniscule mouthful of stew. "When we get to Portreath," she says, "what do we do?"

"You're the one who brought us here. You tell me."

A look of uncertainty passes across her face.

He has no way to help her find her father. The letter is all that was guiding him and that is in her hands now. She must have known his uselessness when she held that knife to his middle and ordered him to take her to Portreath.

She is not bringing him for knowledge. That much is obvious. She is bringing him for protection. Her world is tiny and uninformed. She needs someone to guide her. And right now, miserable, cowardly Asher Hales is all she has.

Being her chaperone, he realises, is right now keeping him safe.

"There was a man who sailed with your father and I," he says, "who took his earnings and built a life in Portreath.

Perhaps we can seek him out for lodgings." When Scarlett doesn't reply, he says: "I wondered if perhaps it was why Jacob chose to escape there. The allure of a familiar face. A friend."

He glances out the window. Rain is splattering the glass. A halo of light glitters around the street lamp.

"You want to escape," says Scarlett.

"Of course."

"Why? I thought this was what you wanted. To go to Portreath with me and find my father. Have him tell you where Avery hid his riches."

"There are no riches," says Asher.

"I don't understand why you're suddenly so certain of that."

"Of course you understand. Sometimes you just awaken and realise the lies have fallen away."

He sees shadows beneath Scarlett's eyes. "You could run," she says after a moment. "Right now. I couldn't catch you."

"I've no money." His eyes drift instinctively to the faint bulge in her bodice where she has buried the pouch of coins. A tiny sum earned from selling smuggled lace. But enough to get him back to Polperro.

Scarlett tugs her shawl across her chest. She pushes her bowl towards him. "You may as well finish it."

He brings the spoon to his lips. "I don't know why there has to be such animosity between us," he says, encouraged by her gift of the leftover stew. "We are both victims. We've both been deceived by Jacob. He left me alone on the beach with the man he murdered. Left you and your brother to carry his debts."

Scarlett doesn't reply. She watches Asher eat. When he has swallowed the last mouthful, she stands abruptly. "We're going upstairs. I need to sleep."

Yes. Sleep, thinks Asher. And he will run.

But when they get to the room, Scarlett pulls a length of rope from her pack and uses it to tie his wrists to the leg of the bed. The knife flashes between her fingers as she knots and binds, as though it has grown a part of her.

Asher watches the blade glint in the candlelight. A swing of his arm and he could knock it from her hands. Knock her to the floor. But mistime the action and she'll have the blade between his ribs in a second. The thought of the pain makes his stomach contract as though he has been struck.

She has knotted the rope tightly. It digs into the skin on his wrists. The humiliation of it makes his insides burn.

Scarlett climbs into the bed and covers herself with the blanket before unlacing her skirts and stays. She blows out the candle and falls asleep quickly.

Asher sits up against the leg of the bed; the only comfortable position he can manage. A glow from the street lamps pushes through flimsy grey curtains. He hears rain patter the roof.

He looks over his shoulder at Scarlett. In sleep, her steely expression is gone. She looks younger, more vulnerable. The heartbroken girl who had curled up against him after Bobby Carter had died.

A thread of dark hair hangs across one eye. Lips parted, skin pale.

He had never felt a great attraction to that hair, that skin, those parted lips. He had just felt a great attraction to the way Scarlett had made him feel worthy. Made him feel better than the rest. She had looked upon him and seen the great man he longed to be. Scarlett Bailey had been a precious thing.

But now her eyes are clouded with anger and she sees him as nothing more than a liar and a coward. Sees him no differently to the rest of the world. And so, it will be a joy to throw her to the revenue men. A joy to take the stand against the woman who has bound him, trapped him, stripped away the last of his self-worth. He will watch that once precious thing be wrapped in chains.

She opens her eyes. Watches Asher without speaking.

"What will you do?" he asks. "If you find Jacob?"

Scarlett doesn't speak at once. "I'll not find him. Because he's dead."

That's what this is journey is about? Proving Asher wrong? Proving the world is as it should be? A cross-county journey to bring sunny Scarlett back?

He waits.

"I don't know what I will do," she says after a moment. "I just want him to see me. I want him to know that I'm aware of what he did to us." Her voice is thick with sleep. "And you?"

He laughs coldly, yanks against the restraints. "I'm not here by choice."

"Jacob tried to pin the murder he committed on you. Don't you want revenge?"

"Is that what you want? You want me to take revenge against your father?"

She rolls over, her back to him. "It doesn't matter," she mumbles. "He's already dead."

"Humour me. We find Jacob alive and well. You discover he abandoned you and your brother in the face of his enormous debt. I put a gun to his head. Do you stop me?"

"No," she says to the dark. "I don't."

SACRED THINGS

Flora is glad for the morning light. Her sleep had been punctuated by dead men and demons. Eyes in the dark and shadows that breathe.

Things she had believed belonged only in fantasy and folklore. But now she is not so sure. Now the solidity of her world is frayed at the edges.

She climbs from the bed and splashes her face at the washstand. The cold water sluices away the last of her nightmares. Pushing back the curtain, she finds a dull, low sun. An empty street. Behind a fringe of trees, the sea is still and purple.

She peeks into her daughter's bedroom. Bessie is breathing deeply and rhythmically, sleeping off what Flora hopes is the last of her illness.

Time to enter the parlour. She has put it off for two days.

She opens the door slowly and draws in her breath. The room is strewn with broken glass; jars shattered across the floor. The chest that had held her mother's herbs and charms lies upended in the middle of the room. A chair is overturned, and dishes lie in pieces beside the leg of the table.

Flora's stomach tightens. The room is a cold reminder of how she had been turned upon by the villagers she had grown up amongst. She is glad her mother is not here to see the way these things she'd held as sacred have been flung so callously around the inn.

Glass crunches beneath her boots. The mob have left some things intact. Her mother's adder stone ring. A watch ball bundled in a cloth. By miracle, the black glass hand mirror. She places scattered herbs back into their pouches and slides everything unbroken into the chest. She latches the lid.

Lock these things away. Don't go near them again.

But she feels an odd reluctance to imprison the trunk back in her mother's room where she had found it. Yes, this venture into the craft had been a dangerous one, but what if it had been the craft that had saved Bessie's life? In desperation, Flora had turned to healing stones and whispered incantations over her sick daughter. The next morning, Bessie had been well. A coincidence? Perhaps. But it now seems far too arrogant to discount the possibility of magic.

Flora runs a finger over the surface of the chest. It is worn soft and smooth by decades of her mother's touch. She can't turn away, she realises. She can't forget. She is the healing woman's daughter. If there is even an ounce of legitimacy to these whispered rhymes, it is up to her to find it.

She takes the chest to her own bedroom and sits it beside the washstand.

"Mammik?" Bessie's voice sounds down the hall as Flora is sweeping the last of the broken jars. She finds her daughter sitting up in bed, tugging at the sheets. "I want to get up."

Flora presses a hand to Bessie's forehead. Cool and dry. Relief floods her.

They sit in the parlour eating porridge in front of a flickering fire. The sun pushes through the windows and burns away the last of the bitterness lingering in the room.

Bessie touches a finger to the strapping on Flora's forearm. "What happened?"

Flora pushes away memories of men dragging her from the inn, of their vicious accusations. Pushes away memories of broken glass and fire and Tom Leach's knife blade. *Bleed the witch.*

"Nothing, *cheel-vean*," she tells Bessie. "Eat your breakfast."

A knock at the door.

Flora finds Charles Reuben on her doorstep. He is dressed in an embroidered waistcoat and pleated blue justacorps, a powdered wig on his head. A black and white dog circles his ankles, entangling him in its rope leash. Flora can't hold back a smile.

"I heard your daughter was unwell," he says. "I thought to see how she is."

"She is much better. Thank you." The dog hurls itself at Flora, pawing at her knees. She bends to scratch its ears.

Reuben clears his throat. "About the dog... I've little time to care for the poor thing. I wondered if perhaps Bessie might do a far better job. If she cares to, of course."

Flora hesitates. The two sides of Reuben make her wary. Beneath this guise of caring, he is the ruthless businessman who has made Isaac and Scarlett's life hell. Still, he has shown Flora nothing but generosity. She can offer him civility in return.

"I'm sure she will love it." She pauses. "Bess is upstairs. Perhaps you might like to give her the dog yourself."

Reuben smiles. "I would like that very much."

Bessie is sitting cross-legged on the couch, her porridge bowl in her lap. The dog strains against the rope when he sees her. She scrambles from the couch and dives onto her knees in front of the dog, ruffling his fur in a fit of giggles.

"He's after a new home, Miss Kelly," says Reuben. "Would you be so kind?"

Flora goes to the kitchen and hangs the kettle over the range.

She hears: "Take him outside twice a day for a good run."

"Oh yes sir. Of course."

Flora hears the tap of claws and Bessie's excited shrieks. She spoons tea into the pot. What would Isaac think if he came to the inn to find Charles Reuben and his dog lounging around her parlour?

Foolish thoughts. It's a pot of tea, not a marriage proposal. Courtesy, not betrayal.

She carries the tea tray into the sitting room. The dog is on the couch beside Bessie, lapping up the remains of her porridge.

Flora hands Reuben a steaming cup. "It seems he has made himself at home."

Reuben smiles. "I'm glad." He sips slowly. "I hear Isaac Bailey and his men are reopening the tunnel."

Flora says nothing. Reuben will find out the smuggling tunnel is complete, of course, when the men use it to land the goods from his next run. But she knows it best that he remains ignorant while Isaac loads the contraband from his own venture later that week.

"It has been reopened," she says shortly. "But Isaac tells me it will not be finished for several weeks or more."

"Perhaps you might allow me to see it some time."

Flora lets her teacup clink against its saucer. "I'd prefer if we spoke of something else, Mr Reuben. I don't wish to discuss the tunnel in front of my daughter."

Reuben nods. He takes another mouthful of tea. "When do you plan to reopen the inn?"

"The windows need fixing."

"Perhaps I could—"

"It's all right," Flora says quickly. "Isaac has already offered to help me. I'll reopen once they're done."

He lowers his voice. "You know we no longer have the protection of the authorities. You risk a visit from the excisemen."

Flora picks up the porridge bowls and hands them to Bessie. "Take these to the kitchen, *cheel-vean*. Give the dog a little water."

Bessie disappears down the hallway, the dog's claws tapping on the floorboards as he scurries after her.

Flora turns back to Reuben. "I have the correct licences," she says.

"One of which is counterfeit."

"I trust you can be relied upon to keep that to yourself."

He sighs. "I regret helping you obtain that liquor licence. Operating with it is trouble."

"Your concern is noted," says Flora. "But I've made up my mind."

He smiles slightly. "You have a determination in you, Mrs Kelly. You remind me of my wife."

"Your wife? I was unaware—"

"I buried her a lifetime ago. With my son. Smallpox took them both."

She meets his eyes. "I'm sorry. Truly."

Reuben walks slowly across the parlour, cup and saucer in hand. He eyes the mantle with its clutter of chipped vases and wax-encrusted candleholders. "I often think of you and your daughter alone in this old place."

Flora shifts uncomfortably. "We are rarely alone, Mr Reuben. This is a public house."

"I worry for you."

"You've no need."

He rubs his freshly shorn chin. "I wish you would reconsider using this forged licence. Run the place as an alehouse."

"Is that why you're here?" Flora asks stiffly. "To talk me out of using the licence?"

"No. I came to offer Bessie my dog."

"You'll lose business," she says after a moment, "if I stop buying liquor from you."

Reuben puts down his cup and meets her eyes. "It's not my business I'm concerned about."

PORTREATH

The light has drained from the day when they arrive in Portreath, the air damp with mist and sea. Wind whips across the water, tunnelling through Asher's buttonholes and stinging his ears.

Revenge, Scarlett had said.

She is wrong. Finding Jacob had never been about revenge. Asher is too old and wise for that. Finding Jacob had been about locating the money and realising his own dreams. Revenge was nothing but a pleasing by-product of the search.

But now he sees the haul is a myth, he has no desire to ever lay eyes on Jacob Bailey again.

Jacob will want revenge of his own. The things Asher had done to him after Albert Davey's death are worthy of revenge, he knows. He had been willing to risk Jacob's wrath when there had been a mountain of silver to uncover. But now he would rather sink into the earth than face the man again.

A part of him appreciates the irony. Asher had groomed and swayed Scarlett to lead him to her father. Now here she is dragging him towards Jacob with a knife to his chest.

Scarlett climbs from the coach and stands at the edge of the road, letting her boots sink into the sludge. She wraps her arms around herself. Her shoulders are hunched, head drooped. In her mud-brown skirts she seems to blend into the bleakness. A duffel bag dangles from her shoulder. "I'm sorry," she mumbles. "This was a mistake. I shouldn't have brought us here. We ought to leave." She fumbles in her pocket for the money pouch.

Asher snorts. No point looking in there. They'd spent the last of the coins securing a ride from Truro.

He begins to walk towards the quay. There will be a tavern close to the water, he is sure. He prays someone in the inn will be able to point him in the direction of his former crewmate. Prays the man will remember him, offer them a bed. His safety from Scarlett's knife blade depends on it.

They walk towards the harbour. Fishing boats knock and sway within the walls of the quay. Sea spray arches and spits as the ocean tries to push its way in. Further out in the bay, two sailing vessels are silhouetted in the last of the light.

Scarlett's eyes dart as she walks. They've travelled, what? Fifty miles? Done nothing more than cross the county. The cobbled lanes of Portreath have much in common with Polperro, yet she is as jittery and uncertain as if she'd been deposited in deepest Africa. Out of her familiar surroundings, she is like a scared cat backed into a corner. Her shoulder bumps against Asher's arm.

Nestled between the cliffs and the quay, a crooked tavern looks to be leaning against the rock. The roof is low and flat, its whitewashed walls peeling. Asher is sure the place will collapse with the next gust of wind.

"Stay here," he tells Scarlett.

She shakes her head. "You're not leaving my sight." Words of fear, not threat.

Asher elbows his way inside. The tavern is a tangle of voices and laughter, wood smoke and tobacco, cursing and breaking glass. Someone bangs loudly on a table. Rugged beams hang low, barely clearing heads. The place reeks of ale and unwashed bodies. Asher's skin prickles.

He makes his way towards the bar, Scarlett treading on his heels. She is the only woman in the place, and heads turn as she passes.

Visiting an old friend, Asher tells the innkeeper.

The man's name?

He hesitates. Richard... What? The name escapes him. He's done his best to push his days of sailing with Jacob and his crew away. He clenches his fist. He'll be damned if he'll blow his cover on account of a bad memory.

"Richard Acton," he says finally, clutching at a faint recollection.

The innkeeper's face falls. "I'm sorry, man. Richard Acton is dead."

"Dead?" Asher tries for a look of grief. Finds himself mourning only his own security. "His widow?" he asks.

"Battery Hill. Third house from the point."

And Asher leads Scarlett out of the tavern, freshly confident he has bought himself a few nights of safety. He will toss a little sympathy towards Mrs Acton and spin a pitiable tale of how the years slide away. For a moment, the churning in his stomach is still. Because if there's one thing he is good at, it is spinning a pitiable tale.

The Actons' house towers above them; a sprawling stone expanse of windows and chimneys. From the front gate they can see down to the quay and over the endless grey plain of the ocean. Scarlett takes it in, wide-eyed and silent.

"The trade was good to him," Asher tells her. There will be plenty he could take from this mansion. Riches he could pocket. Coin to get him back to Polperro and the revenue men.

No. He is not a petty thief. There's a nobility to exposing smugglers, to outing those on the wrong side of the law. He'll not lower himself to their level. He couldn't live with the shame.

"We're leaving," Scarlett says suddenly. She tugs Asher's arm, but he doesn't move.

"Scarlett, come on now. You're exhausted and emotional. There'll be a bed for you here. A hot supper. You need not have anything to do with anyone." His voice hardens. He has the upper hand now. "We're not going marching into the dark with no money and nowhere to sleep." He knocks on the door before she can respond.

When the housemaid answers, he speaks in the silky voice he has perfected. "I'm an old crewmate of Mr Acton. I'm here to see his wife. Pay my respects." And into the house they go.

They wait in a parlour glittering with gilded mirrors and finely embroidered armchairs. A bookshelf stretches from floor to carved ceiling, clutching leather bound volumes that look as if they would crumble if anyone tried to read them. A fire roars in the grate, making Asher's cheeks flush. He looks at Scarlett. She is out of place among such finery, with her patched skirts and tangled tar pit of hair. Still, his gold-rimmed reflection is hardly a picture either after two days stuffed between bales of wet wool and a night at the foot of Scarlett's bed.

Mrs Acton shuffles into the room. She is dressed in a shapeless black mourning gown, grey hair ghosting around her face. Her cloudy eyes light at the sight of guests.

Asher is confident. He can win here. This woman will bend to his charms. "Mrs Acton." He takes her feathery hand. "I'm so sorry for your loss. Richard was a dear friend to me. A great mentor. I'm deeply saddened to hear of his passing."

The old woman's voice is muted and gentle. He has to lean close to make out her words.

Thank you for your kindness.

A pleasure to meet you.

He nods politely at the appropriate places, tosses out false names when the woman asks. He has his story ready. He and Scarlett, brother and sister. The old woman will find them separate rooms. Surely Scarlett will not dare shatter the ruse by creeping into his bedroom to rope him to the floor.

And then before he can say more, he feels her hand at his arm. She sidles against him, digs her fingers hard into his flesh.

"Mrs Acton," she says, honey in her voice, "perhaps you might be so good as to put my husband and I up for the night."

THE DARK

Ready the ship, away from Reuben's eyes. Away from the eyes of Reuben's men.

From Polperro harbour, Isaac can see through the trees to the roof of Reuben's sprawling house on the hill. He cannot see the windows.

Good. He will not be seen from inside the mansion.

Food is loaded onto the lugger. Water. Grappling hooks and rope in case the landing goes awry and they are forced to slip the tubs into the sea.

Cleaning the ship, Isaac will say, if Reuben or his men come looking. Taking care of the vessel entrusted to him. Nothing untoward here.

Tonight they will slide out of the harbour in silence. Isaac realises he is excited. Excited at the deception, at the thought of escape. He has obeyed orders for far too long. Breaking away makes the blood charge hot through his veins.

He dismisses his men. Be back here tonight. Midnight. Silent and ready.

He paces the harbour. Looks through the dark for any sign of the riding officers. Any sign of Scarlett.

Damn her.

He was done with her, he'd told himself, as she had shot accusations at him with a poisonous tongue. But of course, he can no more be done with her than he can be done with one of his children. Not knowing where she is makes him uneasy. She is a firecracker at the best of times. When last he had seen her, she'd been a powder keg waiting to explode.

At the cottage, Caroline is pacing as the baby fusses on her shoulder.

"Has Scarlett returned?" Isaac asks.

"Were you expecting her to?"

Perhaps a part of him had. This is far from the first time his sister has disappeared. Her wild temper has her storming from the house on a regular basis. She and Isaac have fought about everything from bedtimes to potential husbands. But a night's sleep or a mouthful of whisky and she is back to her sunny self. This time feels different.

"I ought to go and look for her."

Caroline plugs a bottle of gripe water into Mary's mouth. "How? You've no idea where to start."

"I can't just do nothing. She could be in danger. She disappeared the same time as that bastard Asher Hales. I don't trust him an inch."

"She's not in danger. She's just being her usual dramatic self."

"You don't know that."

Caroline disappears into the bedroom and lays the baby in the cradle. She pulls the door closed and takes the bottle to the kitchen. "You've a run to make, Isaac. You need to put your mind to it." Her voice sparks. "I'll not lose this chance because of Scarlett."

"What if something's happened to her?"

Caroline marches into Scarlett's bedroom and flings open the storage chest. The lid thuds against the wall. "Her things are gone, Isaac. Nothing has happened to her. She left on her own accord. She left because she doesn't want to be here. And nor do I."

He looks at the empty chest. Is he angry at Scarlett for leaving unannounced, or relieved she has not been taken against her will? His thoughts are cluttered. All he is sure of is his anger at his wife. "How long have you known this?" His voice begins to rise.

She doesn't answer.

"How long?"

Caroline turns away. "Get on the ship, Isaac," she mumbles. "Please. Get us out of this life."

He waits for her to look back at him. Waits for an apology he is sure will not be forthcoming.

Finally, he says: "If Reuben asks after me—"

"You've taken the ship for careening," says Caroline.

"Yes. I know."

He wraps his scarf around his neck and tucks the ends into his coat. When Caroline finally looks up, her face is sunken with regret. She kisses his cheek, holding her lips against his stubbled jaw for a moment. "Be safe."

Isaac gives a short nod and steps out into the street. Light glows through the windows of the Mariner's Arms.

He pushes open the door. A fire roars in the grate, and the sudden change in temperature makes his cheeks burn. Ankers of brandy are lined up along the shelves. He sits at the bar, glancing at the forged liquor licence hanging on the wall. The printer Flora had hired to create it had done a good job. Neat, professional type-setting, a believable replica seal. Nonetheless, the sight of it makes him uneasy.

"Run the place as an alehouse," he had told her, the day he had gone to the inn to fix the broken windows. She had given a dismissive laugh. Told him not to worry for her. All he had been expecting.

She sets a cup of brandy on the bar in front of him. "You're still here."

He sips slowly. "We'll leave at midnight."

"Has Scarlett returned?"

Isaac shakes her head. "I'm worried for her. I think she's with Asher Hales."

Flora smiles. "Then it's Asher Hales you ought to be worried for." There is colour in her cheeks and a shine in her eyes. In spite of his discomfort over the licence, Isaac is glad to see the inn reopen.

She takes a seashell from her collection on the shelf and hands it to him. "Here. It will bring you good luck. Keep you away from Reuben's eyes."

Isaac smiles, running a finger over its silvery surface. He slides it into his pocket. "We could use a little good luck."

Flora takes a half-drunk glass from the bar and empties it into the trough. She wipes her hands on her apron. "I'll leave the cellar unlocked for you."

"No. We'll land in Polperro. Store the goods in the cave."

"Don't be foolish," she says. "You'll use the tunnel."

"I don't want you involved. You've enough to deal with. And there's no telling what Reuben will do if he catches us."

Flora plants a hand on her hip. "I'm not afraid of Reuben. And landing on the eastern beach is far safer than hiding your goods beneath his nose in Polperro." Her blue eyes are piercing. "Am I wrong?"

"No," says Isaac. "But—"

She leans close. Isaac smells brandy and spices on her. "You dug that tunnel. You and my husband. And I know Jack would lose his mind to know you weren't planning on using it to deceive Reuben."

He gives a short laugh. "You're not wrong about that either."

"Of course I'm not." She drops her voice. "Reuben asked about the tunnel. I told him it would not be finished for a time."

"And he believed you?"

"Of course."

Isaac smiles. "You've become a fine liar."

"Well." Her fingers edge toward the cuff of his coat. "I can manage a few lies if it will help you get away. Help you have the life you deserve."

And here is the thought Isaac has been pushing aside since his plans for escape had begun to take shape: leaving Talland will mean leaving Flora. She has always been a part of his life. The pale-haired beauty in the tavern on the hill. He had pulled carts with her, chased balls and hoops, celebrated becoming a husband, a wife, father, mother. Had held her tightly in their shared grief. Isaac can't imagine her not being a part of his life.

But the more contraband he carries into her cellar, the closer the day will come that he leaves her. He knows once he escapes Talland he will never be able to return.

The thought leaves him cold.

She pulls her hand away as though suddenly aware of it. "Tell the lander you'll be coming into Talland. The cellar will be unlocked. Have yourselves a drink when you're done."

Sleep is impossible. Scarlett lies in an enormous wool and feather bed far more luxurious than the lumpy straw pallet she is accustomed to sleeping on. And she stares, wide-eyed at the ceiling.

That evening she had sat through a supper of leathery mutton, listening to Asher regale Mrs Acton with tales of their fictitious marriage. How easily the lies rolled off his tongue, she had thought. She'd forced down a few bites of meat, unsure if it was the pretence of being his wife, or the thought of finding her father that had stolen her appetite.

The food sits heavily in her stomach. She glances down at Asher. He is asleep on the floor, wrists tied to the foot of the bed.

She longs suddenly for the salt-stained hills of Talland. Longs for her sheltered lie of a life where her brother can do no wrong and her father is heroic and gone.

It had been a mistake coming here; a thing she had barely thought through. She had been too angry to look at her brother and so desperate to confront her father that she had not stopped to consider whether she could handle such a thing. Now she is here, she aches for her old, outdated beliefs.

She slides from the bed. Tiptoes past Asher and peers out the window into the mist-streaked courtyard.

It will take her days to get back to Talland on foot. Days of traversing bleak, unknown country. No money for food or shelter.

Beyond the courtyard, a lamp flickers above the door of the stables. Yes. A horse.

She fumbles in the dark for her clothes. She laces her stays crookedly and cannot find one of her garters, but she doesn't care. She takes her pack and tiptoes down the stairs. Out into the stables.

The lamp casts orange light across the hay-lined stalls. Three horses watch with giant eyes. Scarlett slides a saddle from the hook on the wall. Wind gusts beneath the door, making the lamp flicker. She tightens the saddle around the smallest of the horses and swings herself onto its back. She unhooks the lantern and begins to ride the steep hill out of town. Up, up, up. The lights of the village disappear quickly. She can't see the ocean, but hears it writhe and churn against the black rock. A different coast to her own. A different sea. It is wilder here. The lantern flickers, useless against the night. Where is she going? She can barely make out the road.

In the pulsing dark, she can feel them; the spirits of the hills dancing their invisible dance. Her ears strain. Is that their high-pitched laughter on the edge of the darkness? She can't be sure beneath the roar of the sea.

The spirits will take a lonely traveller; Scarlett knows the stories. Disorient him and make him giddy until he has lost all thoughts of where home lies.

And perhaps, Scarlett thinks, perhaps they have her. Because the land has become a maze. She has no sense of the lay of these inky purple hills.

Even if she could find her way back to Talland, what is there for her but outdated stories and broken relationships?

Leaving Portreath won't restore her ignorance. It won't restore her trust in Isaac, or in Asher. It won't return her father to his watery grave. She needs the truth. If Jacob is in Portreath, she needs to know. Needs to confront him. She cannot live a life built on lies and tainted memories.

Rage flies up at her from nowhere. She feels herself fling the lantern without the thought entering her head. Glass shatters; the sound dull against the grassy trail.

With the sudden, violent blackness, her anger vanishes, replaced by shock and fear. She cannot see her hand in front of her face.

The dark has always calmed her, comforted her. But this dark is vast and endless. Inescapable. This is dark that hides burial chambers and runaways and a thrashing, untamed sea. Scarlett hears a murmur of panic escape her. So this is what it is to be afraid of the dark.

The back of her neck prickles with sweat, despite the bitter cold. A few flimsy stars push through the cloud bank; all she has to show her up from down.

She reaches for the horse's mane. Runs a hand through the wiry hair to calm herself. She presses her chest against the animal's thick neck. She needs warmth. Needs to feel another pulse, another being's breath. She feels like the last person left on earth.

The world has become dark and unidentifiable. She has broken away from her family, her home. Fled across the country with a man she no longer trusts. The spirits in the hills could take her now and who would ever know? Perhaps no one would even care.

No one is coming for her. The dark is hers to navigate alone.

THE LIGHT

The morning, Scarlett is sure, will never arrive. Her eyes try to make sense of the darkness. They strain to see the horse she is leaning against, the owl she hears hooting above her head. She tries to decipher the shifting shadows, tries to pull reality from the tangle of her imagination. How many hours has she been here on the hills, her fingers stiff and cold around the horse's reins? Far too many hours to fit into one night, she is sure.

But at last, in a small miracle, the sun does come. It is pale and cold, but it brings light. Exhausted, she takes the horse back to the stables and slips soundlessly into the house. Asher is still asleep when she kicks off her boots and climbs into bed. She is grateful for it.

She wakes several hours later to him rattling the bed frame.

"You can't leave me here all day, Scarlett! I'm not a damn animal."

Reluctantly, she climbs out of bed and unties him. He glances at the rumpled skirts she had slept in.

"You tried to leave." A faint smile turns his lips. "How far did you get without me?"

Scarlett grits her teeth.

Asher relieves himself at the chamber pot. "Mrs Acton will want to know why we didn't come to eat this morning."

"I'm sure you'll talk your way around it." She wrangles her hair into a thick plait and pins it at her neck. Her few hours of sleep have done little to energise her. And being back at the house has not eased her loneliness. She watches Asher rinse his cheeks at the washstand. Water runs down his sharp jaw. Scarlett remembers herself tracing a finger across it, his skin silky, freshly shaven. She is glad, of course, to have awakened to Asher's true nature, but there is something oddly comforting about the memory. A reminder that once she had been far more connected to the people around her than the Wild has made her now.

"Did you ever love me?" she asks suddenly.

Asher combs his fingers through his fair hair. He pulls on his coat. "No. Does that surprise you?"

No, it is no surprise, but his blatant honesty stings. "Did you care for me? Was I ever anything more than a means to finding my father?" She wills herself to stop speaking. She does not want affection from Asher Hales. But she is afraid of drowning alone in the darkness and she will reach out a hand to whoever is closest.

"I cared for you, yes," he says. "You saved my life. I've not forgotten that."

She can see what he is doing. Trying to work his way beneath her frozen shell and secure his safety from the knife at her knee. She has spent enough time around him to become adept at identifying his manipulation. But she needs something to cling to. A raft in the great expanse of the Wild. She hears herself say: "And do you care for me still?"

"I should like to," Asher says pointedly. "But when you are like this, it is a difficult thing."

She watches him lace his boots. There is a faint tremor in his hands, she notices. Beneath his neatly tied hair, the muscles in his neck are rigid.

In all the time he had been in Talland, Asher had never spoken of his family, Scarlett realises. Never spoken of another soul who might have stirred in him something close to affection. And as far as she could tell, no one had come looking for him after his ship had catapulted onto their shore. Asher Hales, Scarlett thinks, is just as lonely as she is. Had he drawn close to her only so he might hunt down Avery's haul? Or had he too needed a raft to cling to?

"Have you ever been in love?" she asks suddenly.

Asher doesn't look at her. "Yes," he says after a moment.

Scarlett feels a strange rush of jealousy. Jealousy towards the woman, no. Jealousy towards Asher himself. She wants to experience love. "Who?" she asks.

He clears his throat. "If you want to leave, we shall. I'm sure we can talk Mrs Acton into giving us a horse or two."

"We're not leaving," she says, forcing steadiness into her voice. "I need to find Jacob."

She walks towards the tavern with the knife at her knee and her hand at Asher's elbow. A grey pall of an evening has settled over the village, mist turning the street lamps into hazy globes of flame. Scarlett pushes her way inside. The front room is noisy and thick with the smell of tallow and pipe smoke. A tall man bumps her elbow, his ale spilling down the front of her skirt. Dampness soaks through a hole in her boot. She shoves her way to the bar, glancing edgily over her shoulder to ensure Asher is still close.

"Jacob Bailey," she says to the innkeeper. "Do you know him?"

Jacob Bailey?, she wants him to say. *That poor fellow is long dead.* Or, even better; *never heard of such a man.*

But instead, he says: "Jacob, ayes. Of course."

Her legs weaken. The man is lying, he has to be. In league with Asher and whoever had written that cursed letter. All part of some twisted game. "Where?" she manages. "Where can I find him?"

The innkeeper scratches his bristly chin. "Lives in that shithole on the northern hill."

Scarlett tries to swallow, but her mouth is dry. Around her, the tavern swims. "The northern hill?"

"Ayes. Make your way out of town. Jacob's is the first cottage you'll come to." His prickly face is suddenly close to hers. "You all right there, maid? Get a shot of brandy into you. Yours for a penny."

Scarlett stumbles away from him, seeking Asher out among the crowd. She has lost sight of him in the sea of sailors' slops and naval uniforms. Faces leer at her; salty beards and pocked cheeks. She looks around dizzily, searching for the door.

A hand is suddenly around her arm. "Steady there, maid."

She looks up. The man's face is lined and leathery. His red velvet justacorps is bare in places, powder on his shoulders from a threadbare white wig. There is an unsettling tattiness to him.

"This is no place for a woman to be alone," he tells Scarlett in a strange, breathy voice.

She looks at his hand, still tight around her upper arm. "Let go of me."

"You don't look well." He takes a glass from the table and presses it into her hand. "Drink this. It'll help."

She looks down at the amber liquid.

"It's brandy. Go on. It'll settle you."

The liquor has a rich, floral scent to it. "This isn't brandy," she coughs.

"Of course it is. Armagnac. Drink up. You'll feel better for it." He presses his hand into the small of her back. Spidery fingers work their way up her spine.

She drops the glass and shoves her way into the street. She leans over the edge of the quay and splashes her face. The seawater is icy, bracing. It brings back a scrap of clarity.

She straightens. Asher is gone. How could she have let such a thing happen? She ought to have left him tethered to the bed where there was no chance of him breaking free. But the thought of entering the tavern on her own had made something twist inside her. Outside of the world she knows, Scarlett has begun to see that she too is a coward.

She hunches by the tavern wall, trying to push away the lingering dizziness. She knows Asher plans to turn she and Isaac over to customs. If he makes it to Polperro without her brother's knowledge, the revenue men will be at their door. For all her anger at Isaac, the thought of him in danger makes panic rise within her.

She tries to steady her thoughts. Asher has no money. No means to make it back. Not yet at least. She has a little time. Time to push Asher Hales to the back of her mind and focus on other, more immediate issues.

The cottage on the northern hill.

She swallows heavily. Stands. Begins to walk towards the edge of the village. Women push past her clutching baskets of fish. A blue and gold carriage waits at the edge of the harbour, the horse nosing Scarlett as she passes.

As she climbs the hill, stillness takes over. Portreath becomes a flicker of light at the water's edge.

Ahead is the tiny cottage, lit only by the moon. It stands a few yards back from the road, rising from tangled gorse and blackberry bushes; a mess of leaning walls and thatching.

Scarlett stares for a moment, breathless from the climb. She had wanted the cottage to be a lie, as she had wanted Jacob to be a lie. She presses her forehead to a lightless window. The dark is too thick to see inside. Abandoned? Yes, it could certainly be abandoned.

Wind whips through her hair, carrying the smell of sea and damp earth. She hears a distant peal of laughter rise from the village.

The undergrowth crackles. Scarlett starts, darting away from the window and hiding in a tangle of trees. She holds her breath. A fox darts across the path and she lets herself breathe.

An abandoned cottage, she tells herself. Owned by a dead man.

A SAFE PATH

With Isaac and his men at sea, the Mariner's Arms is quiet. A cluster of old men sit by the fire, the hiss and crackle of burning logs punctuating their conversation.

Two riding officers arrive, order ales. Since the night of Bobby Carter's death, the revenue men have been a fixture in the area. Flora is glad when they leave.

Late in the evening, a man comes alone to the inn. He has been to her tavern before, Flora is sure. A man from Tom Leach's crew.

He sidles to the bar and takes off his knitted cap. His hair is knotted and colourless, his eyes dark beads in leathery, pitted cheeks. He smells of sweat and old salt.

"You work with Tom Leach," Flora says tautly. "You're not welcome here."

The man climbs onto a stool and tosses his cap onto the bar.

"Your pistol," says Flora. "Give it to me. All weapons to be turned in at the door. House rules."

He snorts. "Since when?"

She folds her arms.

"Don't got no weapons." He eyes the ankers lined up along the shelf. "Last time I were here we was all winking at the kettle."

Flora says nothing.

"You've a licence then. Hard to get your hands on, I hear. Expensive."

"Business is doing well," she says icily.

The man looks around the empty inn. "Don't look to be doing so well. Where's Isaac Bailey and his men? They just made a run for Reuben last week. They can't be at sea again."

"At home, I assume." Flora folds her arms. "Did Leach send you?"

The man shrugs.

She glares at him. "Are you a fool, or are you just acting as one? What does he want? Why has he sent you?"

There can be no good behind the man's visit. Isaac had sent Leach's cutter to the bottom of the river. She is sure he will want retribution.

"He says he's keeping an eye on things," the man tells Flora. "He don't trust none of you. And I'd say he's right not to."

Flora snorts. "Why, because Isaac and his men aren't here? Do you think them a pack of drunkards?"

He chuckles. "Perhaps."

"Why does Leach not come and see me himself?"

"He says you're a witch. He's afraid you'll set the devil on him."

Flora hides a smile.

"Perhaps I'll tell him," the man says slowly, "that Bailey and his men all seem to be missing." He twists his cap into a fat woollen sausage, a crooked smile turning the corner of his lips. "I'm sure Tom would like to know what they're up to."

Flora glances around the tavern. The other customers have left. "I don't know what you're implying," she says coldly, "but whatever it is, I'm sure you're wrong. Now leave. You're mistaken if you think you'll get served in my tavern."

The man considers her, then climbs from his stool and disappears.

The inn is quiet again.

Flora locks the door. She checks the cellar is open and the entrance to the tunnel clear. Then she climbs upstairs.

She opens the bedroom door and peers in at the children. Bessie and Gabriel breathe deeply, backs to each other in Bessie's bed. Mary sleeps in a basket on the floor, tiny pink arms stretched above her head.

Flora finds Caroline in the parlour. She had brought her children to the inn while the tavern's doors were open. Put them to bed so she might go to the cliffs and guide the men home.

Caroline's desperation for escape is glaring. Flora can't remember the last time she had seen her stand on the cliffs with a signalling lantern. In the early days, perhaps, before Gabriel and Bessie. A time of flowing liquor and sunrises.

There is a need in Caroline, Flora sees, to involve herself in Isaac's plans. To oversee the creation of their new life. At the sight of her in the parlour with a lamp in her hand, Flora feels a tinge of nostalgia; half pleasant, half tainted with sorrow.

She has missed Caroline. Still misses her now, though they stand a foot apart. Misses her friendship, her quick-witted, grounded conversation. Her rationality amongst a sea of believers.

Caroline had pulled away after Jack's death, when Flora had needed her the most. She had needed someone to speak to, someone to fill the new silence, the sudden emptiness. Had needed someone who would allow her to fall apart and not make her feel weak.

But Caroline had been unable to look her in the eye. She had been wracked by her own guilt, Flora is sure. A feeling that Isaac had been responsible for the tunnel's collapse.

Flora has never felt such a thing. Never sought to pin blame. It had been nothing but an horrific accident— one that had been as hard on Isaac as it had been on her, she is sure.

She smiles at Caroline, trying for a fragment of the warmth that had once existed between them.

"You'll stay with the children?" Caroline's fingers tense around the handle of the lantern.

Flora nods. "Of course. Go. The men will be back soon."

And Caroline disappears out of the inn, out towards the cliffs with the lantern in her hand. A lantern to alert the men of a safe path to the eastern beach. A safe path to the tunnel beneath the Mariner's Arms.

Flora paces, full of restless energy. A distant, long-ago feeling she remembers from nights waiting for Jack to return home on a ship full of liquor.

Bessie's dog scampers in from the kitchen and circles her legs. She glances at the clock on the hearth. Just past midnight. A sliver of moonlight peeks through a gap in the curtains. Flora pours herself a glass of brandy and drinks it by the window. A dark shadow of birds glides past the glass.

So Tom Leach believes her a witch. He has threatened her over it in the past. And yet it seems his fears are keeping him from the Mariner's Arms. Perhaps his fears are keeping Flora safe.

She puts down her glass and goes to the room that had once been her mother's. Sprigs of mallow leaves and yarrow hang drying from a string she had stretched across the room. She touches one of the fragile fronds.

Not yet dry. Leave them another day.

She stares at the bundles hanging from the ceiling. She had been adamant this would not be her life. She would not surround herself with healing herbs. And yet the sight of the bundled stems begins to settle a restlessness that has existed in her for longer than she has been aware of.

She goes to her bedroom and pulls the black mirror from the chest. She sits cross-legged on the bed and holds the glass face down in her lap. Through the ajar door she can hear the children's deep breathing and the husky snores of the dog.

The room feels vast around her.

A room for two. It had been her grandparents' room. Her parents'. Hers and Jack's. She feels a stab of deep loneliness.

She turns over the mirror. Sees her own faint reflection; pale hair falling in pieces over her cheeks, stark against the dark of the mirror. Sees the soft contours of her face in the glass.

Flora sees she is becoming her mother.

She hears in her head:

Watch, cheel-vean. *Patience.*

And she watches. Is patient.

Because no longer can she brush away her mother's craft as a fairy tale. No longer can she pretend to be so knowing, so wise. The more she sees, the less she understands.

She watches the glass. And there are images. Men running in the dark. Where is she seeing them? In her mind's eye? In the glass? She is unsure. Is this anything more than imagination?

Quiet. Stop thinking. Let the images come.

Horses. Guns. A man in blue lies sprawled on his back, staring blankly at the night sky.

The cellar stairs creak loudly. Flora throws the mirror on the bed, a strange tightening in her chest. Another creak of the stairs. It is too early to be Isaac and his crew, surely. The dog scampers and barks.

She hurries down to the bar. The cellar door is hanging open.

And Flora thinks of dead men walking the lightless tunnel.

She hates that this is where her thoughts go now. Hates that her mind grabs first at superstitious tales. Hates that she cannot have healing herbs without having ghosts as well.

She stops at the top of the cellar stairs. Silence now. Even the mice are still.

The quiet had bothered her the most after her husband had died. Somehow, the silence had seemed more profound when she knew she'd not be woken by his footsteps on the stairs at dawn after a run.

She steps into the cellar. As a girl, she had been afraid of the inn's creaks and shadows. Her imagination had populated the empty rooms with a colourful cast of fairies and knockers. Shadowy spirits hiding beneath the beds.

She feels that old childhood fear pushing at the edges of her rationality. She is suddenly acutely conscious of the expanse of the building around her; the upstairs rooms filled with the belongings of her dead family, the empty bar, the cluttered cellar, the lightless tunnel reaching for the sea.

And she longs suddenly for the simplicity of childhood. If only she could believe the noise from the tunnel to be the doing of fairies and knockers. Because this cellar, this tunnel, is no longer the hideout of imaginary beings, it is the site of her husband's sudden and horrific death.

She does not believe in ghosts. And yet, since Isaac had prised the tunnel open, she has felt herself drawn towards it. Felt herself making for the dark, searching for what might hide within. Searching for the boundaries of the world she has trained herself to know.

The lamplight falls on a tiny figure at the mouth of the tunnel.

"Bessie?" calls Flora.

Her daughter mumbles unintelligibly.

The lantern Flora has lit for the men sways as a draught sighs through the tunnel. Shadows flicker over broken furniture.

Bessie is standing in her nightshift, staring into the dark passage. "Tasik," she says.

Flora's breath catches. She touches her daughter's shoulder. Bessie starts, whirls around.

"What are you doing down here, *cheel-vean*?"

Bessie looks at her mother with bewildered eyes. "I don't know."

Flora kisses the side of her head, trying to slow her own racing heart. "You must have come down here in your sleep." She takes her daughter's hand. "Let's go back upstairs."

And with Bessie in bed, Flora finds herself back in the cellar, shining the lantern into the mouth of the tunnel. She hears Bessie's voice in her head.

Tasik.

My father.

Flora hears herself say: "Jack, are you there?" Her arms prickle. She is afraid, she realises. Afraid of what? Her husband?

No. Afraid she might find proof. Afraid she might see or hear something that might tilt her world to the point of no return.

Silence, she thinks. Let there be silence.

For all she would give for another minute with Jack, she can think of little worse than hearing his voice echoing through the tunnel's twists and turns.

But there is not silence. There are footsteps. Faint voices and the thud of barrels. Flora exhales sharply at the solidity of the sounds.

The noise grows louder, accompanied by streams of orange light.

Here are the men, spilling from the tunnel with dusty cheeks and windswept hair. A barrage of footsteps; the landing party and the crew, chuckling, demanding whisky.

"Whisky, ayes," she tells them. "It's waiting for you upstairs."

John Baker plants a bristly kiss on her cheek. "Bless you, Flora."

Isaac is the last man out. "We've left the ankers in the tunnel. Better way they're hidden there than have them sitting in your cellar." He rolls the empty barrels across the room to hide the tunnel's entrance.

Impulsively, Flora throws her arms around his neck. His hands slide around her waist, holding her to him. She can smell the sea on his skin.

"What's happened?" he asks, his voice muffled by her hair. "Are you all right?"

"Nothing's happened. Glad you're back safe is all." Suddenly embarrassed, she tries to pull away, but Isaac keeps her close.

"You'd tell me, wouldn't you?" he says in Cornish. "If you weren't all right?"

She can't remember the last time she heard him speak their language. English, always, for Caroline's benefit.

He steps back and looks her in the eye. "Flora? Would you tell me?"

"*Heb mar*," she says. "Of course." Her voice feels stuck in her throat.

"Good."

She unhooks the lantern from above the stairs. "He's a good thing then, your agent?"

"Seems it, ayes."

She thinks to tell him of the visit Leach's crewmate had paid her. No, she decides, she will not bring him down. Instead, she says: "I'm glad. You'll have escaped this place before you know it."

Isaac says nothing.

"You don't seem so taken with the idea."

"I'll miss you, is all."

Flora's throat tightens. She has not let herself feel anything other than happiness for Isaac at the thought of his escape. She will miss him too, of course. Deeply, desperately. Cannot bring herself to think how it will feel to walk past his cottage and see it empty. To open the inn's doors and know he will not be striding in for a drink. She cannot allow herself such selfish thoughts.

But Isaac's admission brings a heaviness to her chest. His escape will be final, absolute. She knows once he leaves Talland they will never see each other again.

Unable to look at him, she lets her gaze drift upwards to the footsteps thudding above their heads. The landing party's footsteps. Caroline's footsteps.

Flora manages a nod. *Yes, I'll miss you too.* She knows it does not need to be spoken.

But things must change. Isaac must break free. Their past in Talland must become nothing more than memory.

INDIRECTION

After escaping Scarlett, Asher manages a few hours of sleep in the doorway of the cobbler. He wakes with an ache in his back and his skin itching with filth.

Look where his life has taken him. He hasn't felt this worthless and low since his days of servitude in New England.

He makes his way towards the harbour, stretching his neck from side to side as he walks. He kneels at the edge of the sea and splashes his face. The chill of the water wakes him, but leaves his skin sticky. He feels the patchy beginnings of a beard.

He tucks in his dirty shirt. Perhaps this dishevelled, earthy look will make him seem more amenable to physical labour.

He asks at the fishing port. No work available. Tries three farms on the hill before finding a man willing to hire him to muck out his stables.

Asher rubs his jaw. "When will you pay me?"

"End of the week."

Something about the farmer sets Asher on edge. Perhaps the constant shifting of his eyes, or the way his long fingers ripple as though they've a life of their own. The man's breeches are riddled with holes, his coat encrusted with dirt. What a sorry thing, Asher thinks, that he might take orders from such a creature.

His thoughts are an endless rattle of paranoia. Each man he has passed, he has thought to be Jacob Bailey. He needs to leave this place as soon as possible.

He takes the position.

The farm is a miserable patchwork of fields on the edge of the village. The house is bare and has with far too much in common with the barn for Asher's liking. The sleeping quarters smell vaguely of animals and the tin roof rattles when the wind blows. As far as Asher can tell, he is the only employee.

Pay in a week. He can manage to shovel shit and avoid Scarlett for a week. And when the money is in his pocket, he will return to Talland, via the Polperro customs house. What a pleasure it will be to watch from the cliff as the revenue men swoop.

His pockets will finally be full when he will go to that cottage door.

I'm sorry, he will tell Caroline. And he will mean it. Because once they had sat by the fireside with their legs intertwined and planned a better life. Once, he had looked over his brandy glass and told her he loved her. Once, he had thought that returning to England would mean returning to her.

I'm sorry, Callie, he will say, as the revenue men haul away her husband and tear that creaking cottage to pieces.

I'm sorry you couldn't see me for the man I was always destined to be. I'm sorry for your most terrible of choices.

"My husband is unwell," Scarlett tells Mrs Acton at breakfast. "No, there's no need to disturb him. He's sleeping."

She takes a bowl of porridge upstairs to the bedroom.

"Are you sure I can't fetch the healer?" the old woman calls after her.

Scarlett forces a smile. "That won't be necessary. He'll be up and out of bed tomorrow, I'm sure of it."

And she would be up and out of the house tomorrow. This ruse, she is sure, will not last another day.

She empties the porridge out the window and paces across the bedroom. Damn Asher Hales to Hell. If she ever sees him again, she will tear out his eyes.

She leaves the house hurriedly. She has no money. Nowhere to go. No sense of where home lies among this vast expanse of hill and sea.

She has always hated being a burden to her brother. Before things had fallen apart between them, she had tried to please him, tried to prove her worth, her helpfulness. But the truth of it is heavy on her shoulders. Without Isaac, she is lost.

She walks towards the water. The edges of the beach are hemmed by jagged cliffs, rock islets rising from the waves. Venture closer and she is sure she will find a coastline pocked with caves and grottos; a warren of dark hiding places.

And Scarlett realises she is not lost. Her world may have been turned upside down, the sea on the wrong side of her, but she is still deep in a world of free trade. Pace this beach at midnight and she is sure she will see a flash of blue from a signalling pistol. See a line of boats sliding through the moonlight.

Stay or go, she needs money. She cannot sew, can barely cook and clean. Her writing is messy and her reading slow. But slip a signalling lantern in her hand and she'll see a trader safely to shore.

Her world.

How best to infiltrate the Portreath ring? Watch the beach and wait? No. It might be weeks before a run is scheduled. She needs to find the men involved. Convince them to slide a little of their wealth into her hands.

She eyes the inn leaning against the cliff. No doubt the traders spend their time in such a place. She will return tonight.

She begins to walk faster along the beach. One end to the other, her boots sinking in the sand. She is directionless still for now, but buoyed by her plan.

By the time the tavern opens in the late afternoon, her stomach is rumbling and her hands are numb with cold. She doesn't look about her as she enters. Doesn't want to know it if the man with the powdered wig is here.

The smile on the innkeeper's face tells her he recognises her.

"D'you find him, then?" he asks. "Jacob?"

She leans across the bar to speak under her breath. "Who runs the trade here?"

"There is no trade."

Scarlett stares him down.

After a moment, he says: "Why are you asking?"

"I need money."

The innkeeper chuckles. "There are other ways a girl like you can earn a few shillings."

Scarlett flushes. Feeling the man's eyes on her, she yanks her cloak closed. "I want work with the smugglers. Hawking. Or a lookout. Whatever they need."

"You want work?" A man's voice behind her.

Scarlett whirls around. The man is young; no more than a few years older than her. Hair the colour of dark coffee hangs over one eye in waves. He is dressed in sand-coloured breeches and a blue broadcloth coat. His arms are folded across his chest.

Scarlett swallows. "Ayes. Hawking. Or—"

"Or a lookout. Yes. I heard you." He eyes her, considering. His lips twitch. "Come with me."

He leads her to the back room of the inn. The tables are crooked and scratched, the fire unlit. The room smells of tobacco and piss. Scarlett shivers.

"You're cold," says the man.

"I'm all right." She eyes him curiously. Is a man so young the leader of their syndicate? She thinks of creaky old Charles Reuben. The man in front of her is slim and muscular, his face unlined and flushed with youth. Perhaps his father had led the ring.

"Is there work?" she asks, her voice trapped in her throat. She pulls back her cloak to reveal the pockets stitched on the inside. "I know what I'm doing. I've been running goods since I were seven years old. Never been caught."

The man digs his hands into the pockets of his coat. "There's no work. We don't need more hands. Stay away from this place."

She raises her eyebrows. "Then why bring me back here?"

"Best to keep our business away from the ears of the landlord."

Impulsively, Scarlett takes a step closer. She can smell musk soap on him. "You could always use more hands." She keeps her voice low. Meets his eyes. "More hands make things easier. Faster."

His lips part.

"You've a landing party full of fisherman, I'm sure," she says. "Men who are clumsy when you take them off a ship. I'm fast and I'm quiet. And I'll do it for cheap."

"You seem quite knowledgeable on such things."

"Does that surprise you?"

"And quite persistent." The man tilts his head, considering. The intensity of his gaze makes Scarlett's cheeks hot.

"Why should I trust you?" he asks after a moment.

She manages a smile. "I don't trust you either. But I'm sure we can do this without a great deal of trust. What are you paying your landing party for delivery? Ten percent? I'll do it for five. And I'll do it twice as fast."

The man rubs the dark stubble on his jaw.

She takes another step towards him; close enough for her skirt to graze the edge of his boots. Close enough to see the slatey blue grey of his eyes. She sees him swallow heavily and feels a faint flicker of satisfaction. His landing party, she is sure, does not elicit such a reaction from him.

"What do you say?"

"Very well," he says finally, huskily. "You'll meet me on the beach tomorrow night. There's a stash of tobacco needs delivering. Consider it a trial."

Scarlett smiles crookedly, looking up at him until she sees a twitch in the corner of his lips. "Tomorrow night," she agrees. "You'll not be disappointed."

THE REALM OF FAIRY TALES

Flora wakes thinking of Jack. She reaches a hand out of
her blankets and feels for his tobacco box that sits on her
nightstand. She holds it close, running her fingers over its
worn wooden engravings. She feels a swell of love. And for
the first time, a grief that is gentle, not breathtakingly sharp.
For the first time, when she thinks of Jack, there is a smile
on her lips instead of pain in her chest. She is surprised by it.

She dresses and goes to the drawer in the parlour for a
ring of keys.

Three former guest rooms line the hall, each clutching the
belongings of her departed family. Her mother's room
cleared, for better or worse. The next of the untouched
shrines; her husband's.

Time now, yes. Time for Jack to live on through his
daughter, through memories of their life together. Not in a
locked and darkened room. And not through ghostly
memories of his death.

With the morning light, Flora sees her behaviour in the tunnel had been foolish. Sees the dark's ability to take away reason.

She slides the key into the lock.

Time now, yes, but her stomach still turns as she pushes open the door. She goes first to the window. Pushes back the curtains and wrenches it open. A stream of cold air blows in.

The wardrobe is open a crack. Flora had sent Scarlett inside to find clothing for Asher Hales, the night he had washed up upon their shore.

Inside the cupboard, she finds Jack's breeches, long sailor's trousers, a woollen waistcoat. Everything is hanging neatly, creaseless and buttoned.

Two days after his death, she had torn his things from the wardrobe in their bedroom to be hidden away in here. Hanging his clothing so carefully had felt like the last thing she could ever do for her husband. The pain of it had been a crushing weight she was sure she would never crawl out from. She had never imagined her grief might work itself into this soft, delicate thing that is pushing around inside her chest.

She slides a shirt from the hanger and squeezes it between her fingers. The linen is patchy and thin. It smells of mildew and moths; a reminder it has been many days and nights that her husband has been gone.

Many days and nights since she had watched Jack's eyes crinkle when her mother had spoken of her craft.

And even longer since Flora had sat opposite him at the supper table and lied. "No," she had said, her head overflowing with herbal remedies and incantations. "I know nothing of it. I've never gone near such things."

Why had she felt a need to hide it? Fear of mockery? No. She knows Jack would have accepted whatever eccentricities she had dropped at his feet.

The lies had come from her own inability to accept her roots. Her embarrassment at the superstitious haze that hung over her family's inn.

She had been ashamed at how small her world was. She'd not left Cornwall until the age of twenty, when Jack had taken her east to show his new wife off to his family. And Flora was determined not to be paraded as an ignorant west country simpleton. She would not be pigeonholed as the Cornish girl with sandy boots and a head full of magic rhymes.

I've never gone near such a thing.

The floor creaks. Bessie stands in the doorway in her nightshift. "Tasik's room," she says.

The dog scampers inside, nose to the floor. Flora folds the shirt and sits it on the bed. "Bessie, take your dog. He's getting under my feet."

"*She*, Mammik. It's a girl dog."

"I don't think so, Bess."

"It is. I named her Molly."

Flora smiles.

Bessie scoops the dog into her arms. "The room," she says. "It smells like him."

Yes, Flora can smell it too. That faint scent of pipe smoke and boot polish beneath the dust and damp of two lightless years.

She piles the clothing on the bed, pushing past the faint ache in her chest. She needs to do this. Needs to release the past before she ends up chasing more shadows into the dark.

"Bessie," she says carefully. "You were in the tunnel last night. Do you remember?"

Her daughter looks at her quizzically. Shakes her head.

"You were talking to someone. You don't remember who?"

"No."

Flora places the wearable clothing in a trunk for the charity collection. She takes Jack's books from the shelf. Sifts through the pile to find his favourites and puts them aside for the bookshelf in the parlour. The rest she places into the trunk. She takes a silver compass from the shelf and slides it into her pocket. "A dream," she tells Bessie. "Nothing more, I'm sure."

She needs it to be nothing more.

She latches the trunk and carries it into the hallway. A waft of drying mallow leaves comes from the room that had once been her mother's.

This venture with the mirror, with healing herbs, she would never have done if Jack had been alive. She would have lived by her husband's beliefs, the way she had lived by her mother's before she had married. As a child, it had just been assumed she would one day take over the role of village healer. A thing she had never thought to question. The first pangs of doubt she'd felt as a teenager had come as a shock. What if there was no truth to magic? What if she had grown up believing in fairy tales? At first, she could not believe she had even dared think such blasphemous thoughts.

She had only just begun to explore the edges of her own beliefs when Jack had bowled into her life, sending healing charms to the realm of fairy tales.

Flora looks at the two cleared rooms, doors swinging open, side by side. She had loved them both so dearly; her husband, her mother. Loves so blinding she had taken their beliefs and made them her own.

She would give her life to see either of them again. And yet she can't help but think who she might begin to be without them.

A RUNNING OF ERRANDS

The tunnel is filled with brandy ankers. Now Isaac needs buyers. A new impatience is stirring inside him.

"Get your coat," he tells his son. "We'll have you a sailing lesson."

Gabriel's eyes light. He pulls on his coat and bounds out of the house.

They'll sail to Fowey. A larger village, outside of Reuben's control. They'll buy food from the market and pitch from the ship chandler and this will seem nothing more than a running of errands. But Isaac's eyes will be open, his ears alert for the right buyers, the right businesses, the men with money itching to be spent.

Gabriel runs excitedly along the cliff path, reaching the harbour and bouncing onto the lugger ahead of his father. "High tide," he announces. "Westerly wind."

Isaac smiles. "Good."

He is glad his son has taken to the sea. The sea is changeable and challenging but it makes the world accessible. A life on the ocean will show Gabriel new lands, new lives. A world far greater than this oppressive pocket of Cornwall.

The sun is streaking the clouds as they slide from the harbour. Isaac stands on the edge of the foredeck, letting Gabriel take the wheel. The lugger settles into a steady rhythm. He points to a strip of pale sand between jagged rock. "See there. Lantic Bay."

"Is it a landing beach? A hiding place?"

For all he has tried to keep his son blind to it, Isaac knows Gabriel is coming to see the world through smuggler's eyes. The caves are hideouts, the lugger a running vessel, the men in blue and gold, mortal enemies. Impossible, Isaac has realised, to keep his boy shielded from a thing so embedded in the landscape.

"Not a landing beach. A sheltered bay. Safe water. A good sailor ought to know his coast."

But this will not be his son's coast, of course. They will be gone from this place soon. Gabriel's coast will be a puzzle of new coves and Mary will take her first steps in a house without smuggled tea beneath the beds.

Isaac squints as sun reflects off the water, turning the sea translucent blue. "There'll be new places to sail soon," he says. "The Irish Sea perhaps. Or the Scottish Islands. Does that excite you?"

Gabriel nods, smiles his father's smile. Isaac reaches over his shoulder to steady the wheel as it lurches on the swell. He tells stories of his own travels; the turquoise seas of Spain and the fragrant syrup air of the East Indies.

"The East Indies are a long way from Talland," Gabriel says.

"Ayes."

"How far?"

"Near ten thousand miles. Four months at sea or more."

Gabriel says nothing, just looks out across the water. Wondering, perhaps what he might see, if he stayed on the lugger and let the sea carry him for four months or more.

Isaac brings the lugger into Fowey harbour. A large cutter sways on the river, its hull and bare masts painted black.

It is a ghost ship, Isaac is sure. A phantom of the cutter he himself had sent to the bottom of the river.

They are close to Tom Leach's trading territory. Polruan lies on the other side of the river.

There has been a rivalry between the two smuggling rings for as long as Isaac can remember, but there is a new intensity to it now. He can't deny it is part of what had drawn him to Fowey. There is something pleasant about stealing Leach's business as he buys his family's freedom.

Leach is loading a dinghy with unmarked crates. Isaac hurries past, a protective hand on the back of Gabriel's neck.

"Good afternoon to you too, Bailey," calls Leach.

Isaac keeps walking.

"Who is that, Tasik?"

"No one of any importance."

Gabriel looks back over his shoulder. "His ship is black. Is he a pirate?"

"Something like that."

"It's a fine ship, ayes?" Leach calls, leaping from the dinghy and jogging along the harbour to catch them.

Gabriel squints. Gives a faint nod.

"My old cutter, she met with foul play." He looks sideways at Isaac. "This one, she's better. Bigger. Holds more men. More cargo."

More men? Is Leach seeking to expand his syndicate? No doubt he seeks to steal business from the Talland free traders. Let Leach and Reuben fight amongst themselves, Isaac thinks. Whichever man loses, it will be a fine thing.

Leach rubs his dirty beard. "What are you doing in these parts, Bailey?"

"That's no business of yours."

"This is our river. What happens on it is my business. And whatever you're up to, I'm sure it's untoward."

"Untoward," Isaac snorts. "You're a fine one to speak of such things. I'm giving my son a sailing lesson. Nothing more."

Leach chuckles. Turns to Gabriel. "You taking over your grandfather's debts, boy?"

"No," he says, "I'm going to go sail in the Irish Sea or the Scottish Islands or—"

Isaac's fingers tighten around Gabriel's shoulder. He stops talking hurriedly.

Leach smiles to himself.

Isaac ushers his son away from the harbour. The back of his neck prickles. He slides a handful of coins from his pocket and hands them to Gabriel. "I need you to go to the market."

The boy's shoulders fall. "I want to come to the ship chandlers." He looks at Isaac pleadingly.

"The market first. Your mother wants currants and cinnamon. She's to make you heavy cake."

Gabriel's eyes light. "Heavy cake?"

Isaac ushers him towards the market. "I'll meet you at the chandlers when you're done."

"Where are you going?"

"I've someone to see."

Isaac watches Gabriel disappear into the winding streets.

He'll try The Ship, The Well House. A quick word to the innkeeper.

Fine brandy. A good price.

And then he'll hurry back to the market and take Gabriel to the ship chandlers for the pitch. An innocent domestic errand. His son will know this to be nothing more.

He goes to the Well House. He's drunk in the place before. Knows the innkeeper a friendly man with an eye for a good deal.

He is blunt, deliberate. "I've a shipment of brandy looking for a buyer." He brings a vial of liquor from his pocket and plants it on the bar. The innkeeper; a broad-shouldered man in his forties, uncorks it. Inhales.

"Cognac," Isaac tells him. "Fine stuff."

The innkeeper takes a swig. Nods approvingly. "How much you got?"

"Forty ankers. I'll do you a good price. What's Leach charging you?"

The innkeeper eyes him. "How do you know I'm buying from Tom Leach?"

Isaac shrugs. "He trades out of Polruan. It makes sense."

The innkeeper considers. "I'll take twenty ankers. Pay you a pound apiece."

Isaac hesitates. The price is low. He'd been hoping for more. But agree to a pound and he'll secure the sale. He nods. "A pound apiece. But I'll not make the delivery here. You're too close to the customs station. I'll bring them to Lansallos Cove in two days' time. Meet me there."

The innkeeper chuckles. "Had to be a catch at such a price."

Isaac leans forward. "This is a good deal, man. You just bring a wagon. My men will load it for you, cover it. Nothing for you to do but ride home again."

The innkeeper nods finally. "Very well. Lansallos Cove. Twenty ankers at a pound apiece."

Isaac nods. Gives the man's hand a firm shake.

The sun is staining the water as they make their way back to Talland.

Gabriel looks towards the orange horizon. "Tasik," he says, "where is Aunt Scarlett?"

Isaac doesn't answer at once. He's managed to push his sister to the back of his mind, a place she has not been since before he had taken her from the children's home. There is something liberating about washing his hands of her plight. He'd said little to Gabriel to explain her absence. Can't blame him for his curiosity.

"Aunt Scarlett needs a little time away," he hears himself say. And suddenly she is back in the forefront of his mind, jostling his son and daughter for space.

Twenty ankers at a pound apiece is a good start. Two tickets out of Cornwall. Perhaps three. Sell the second half of the haul at a higher price and he'll have enough for his family to leave. Once the money is in their hands, he knows Caroline won't wait. Won't sit around waiting for Reuben to catch them.

Won't sit around waiting for Scarlett to show herself.

Another successful sale and Talland will be a memory. Isaac follows Gabriel's gaze towards the horizon. Wills his sister to come home before there is no home for her to return to.

THE TOBACCO CAVE

Scarlett spends the day walking Portreath; memorising the maze of alleys and the indented footprints worn across the cliffs. She takes in the location of the customs station, finds huers' watch houses on the cliffs that might provide cover for the riding officers. Making a delivery in this foreign place will be a challenge, but she is determined to succeed.

When the light has faded to nothing, she waits on the beach. The sea rolls and pushes at the edge of the cliffs. White water glows at the base of the rock stacks. The last of the fishing boats slide back into the quay, their lights bobbing in a moonlit sky.

Scarlett touches the knife at her knee. There is something comforting about the feel of it against her stockings.

She turns as lamplight spills over the beach. The young man from the tavern comes towards her, his footsteps sighing in the wet sand.

Scarlett stands, her heart quickening. "You're alone."

Wind blows the messy waves of his hair back from his face. Light flickers on the sharp line of his jaw. "The rest of the party will be here shortly. You're early. The men are rarely on time."

"Where do you need me to go?"

"There's a farm at North Cliffs. You'll find the man's name on his gate. Williamson."

Scarlett nods, feeling a swell of relief. She knows the place. She will make the delivery easily. Quick and silent. "And I'll be paid?"

He nods, his eyes meeting hers. "As promised."

She gives him a faint smile. Tonight, she will have money from the traders in her hands. She will be able to afford a bed away from Mrs Acton's. Or a coach ride home.

Thoughts of her father push their way inside her head. She shakes them away hurriedly. There is no place for him here now. No place for him here, ever.

The man nods towards a cave hidden in the cliffs. "You'll make your delivery now. The men will make theirs when they arrive." He leads her through the shallow water. The sea swells around her ankles, filling her boots.

The man shines the lamp into the chasm. A wooden chest sits at the back, protected from the tide. He points towards it. "The tobacco is in the top."

Scarlett steps inside and opens the lid. A fragrant, wrapped package sits above larger bundles she guesses are silk or lace. She takes the tobacco and slides it into her cloak. The light disappears suddenly as the man steps out of the cave. Scarlett stumbles back to the beach. And her mouth goes dry.

He stands at the edge of the water with a pistol in his hand. She freezes, several feet away, the sea knotting her skirts around her calves.

He raises the gun. "Give me the tobacco."

"You don't work with the traders," Scarlett says bitterly. "You work with the revenue men."

The man keeps the gun trained on her. "The tobacco."

She tosses it on the sand. "A fine cover. Are you proud of yourself?"

"No. Not really."

"Good. Nor should you be."

He picks up the tobacco and slides it into his pocket. "What's your name?"

She sighs and trudges out of the water. "Scarlett Bailey." She swallows heavily.

A criminal, just like her father.

But if this scheming revenue officer knows anything of Jacob, he does not let on.

"This way, Miss Bailey," he says, gesturing to the top of the beach with the nose of the gun.

"I'm not going anywhere with you."

"Never been caught, you say. It shows. Here's how things are. You will come with me to the customs station or I am well within my rights to use force."

His calm, even voice is infuriating. Scarlett clenches her hands into fists inside her cloak. He has a pistol. Let the Wild out here and she'll end up with a bullet in her chest.

He leads her up the beach towards the lamp-lit building close to the harbour. Her palms prickle. In all her years in the trade, she has never truly considered what it might be like to be caught. There have been close calls, for certain; the riding officers the night of Bobby's death, the revenue cutter

Asher had sent on their trail. From each, she had walked away with little more than a racing heart.

But now, with a pistol at her shoulder and a riding officer's breath hot on her neck, a prison cell feels frighteningly close. Her legs are unsteady beneath her.

He pushes open the door. And in she goes to the customs house, her feet sliding in wet boots as she walks the gloomy stone corridor. Wooden doors line each side.

The officer leads her into a small room and gestures to a chair at the table. The room smells of old pipe smoke and boot polish.

He sits opposite her, their eyes meeting. She wants to strike him. Wants to snatch that pistol from his hand and pull the trigger. She clenches her teeth until the violent thoughts recede.

"You took the tobacco from here and planted it," she says bitterly. "You set me up."

He nods. "Yes. I'm sorry."

"No you're not."

He eyes her curiously. "You're not from these parts, are you. If you were, I'm sure our paths would have crossed before. Have you come to Portreath to engage in smuggling?"

"You heard what I told the innkeeper. I just need the money."

"Why?"

"To get home."

"Where is home?"

Scarlett shifts uncomfortably. She does not like how closely he is looking at her. What might he see?

"Why the interrogation?" she snaps. "Why not save us both the trouble and just arrest me?"

"I'm not going to arrest you."

She eyes him curiously. "You're not?"

"No. I lied to you. Misled you. It would hardly be the decent thing to do."

Scarlett snorts. "I didn't think you people were bothered with decency."

"Besides," he says, pushing past her comment, "I'd have to pay for the trial out of my own pocket if I were to take you to court. It's better for both of us that I let you go with a warning." He keeps his face even. "I meant it when I said you ought to leave this place, Miss Bailey. And you certainly shouldn't be involving yourself with the smugglers on this coast."

"I'm not afraid of smugglers."

"I can see that. And it may well be your downfall. Violence among smuggling gangs has been on the rise recently. And the men running the ring here are also involved in illegal impressment."

Scarlett raises her eyebrows. "So I'm to fear they'll throw the king's shilling into my ale and cart me off to serve the navy?" She gives a cold laugh. "I don't think so." She knots her hands into her cloak. "If you know who these men are and what they're doing, why not arrest them?"

"I've no proof," he says simply. "But I know they're dangerous. I'm sure you believe you can handle them, but they would have no issue with taking advantage of a young woman like you."

Anger prickles the back of her neck. She has spent her life around free traders. Can hold her own against men like Tom Leach. She doesn't need this man's misguided protection. She just needs money in her pocket.

"You don't know me," she hisses. "You don't know what I can handle." She hears a tremor in her voice. Curses herself for it. But the thought of being alone and penniless is a weight upon her shoulders. "May I leave?" she asks icily.

The officer nods. "Find another way to earn the money you need, Miss Bailey. If I catch you anywhere near the tavern again, I will happily pay for that trial."

THE PAUPER'S BOY

Isaac and Will Francis crouch in the tunnel, a pool of lamplight spilling over the ankers in front of them. A barrel of water sits beside the liquor, ready to dilute the over-proofed spirits.

One part water, four parts brandy. Isaac is careful to ensure his shipment matches that in the vial he had given the innkeeper at the Well House. One part water, four parts brandy. A profitable mix and one that will not sear the throats off its drinkers.

When the brandy is diluted and ready for shipment, they climb upstairs for a celebratory drink.

"You know this is dangerous, ayes?" says Will, sitting beside him at the bar. "Leach won't appreciate you taking his business."

"All the more reason to do it." Isaac empties his brandy, orders another. He gulps from the second glass, seeking the bliss of drunkenness. His mind races with thoughts of secret smuggling runs, then charges into thoughts of Flora.

He swallows hurriedly. These thoughts are the deadly ones. The ones that most need drowning in moonshine.

His mind is full of her. When he closes his eyes, he sees nothing but blonde hair, freckled skin, deep sea blue eyes.

She has been there always, hovering on the edge of his consciousness. Ever since their days of paddling in their underclothes while one of their mothers watched from the beach.

Why does he think of her now with such intensity? Is it the thought of leaving? The knowledge that when he finally escapes Talland, he will leave her here among the liquor and lamplight and never see her again?

She has always been a few rungs above him on the social ladder; his family elbow-to-elbow in their cottage while hers lost themselves in the echoing passages of the Mariner's Arms.

He'd thought of marrying her once, when he'd returned from sea as a young man. When he had first imagined himself breaking free of Reuben's shackles, it was Flora beside him in the escape vessel. But he'd had nothing to offer her. It had been no secret that her mother had looked down on him, believed him unworthy. He was nothing but the pauper's boy who'd once flashed her his arse while his mother's back was turned.

And then there was Caroline. Then there was Jack. His attraction to Flora had been pushed to the background. Buried under years of friendship and marriage to a woman who has no family to judge him.

He realises he is watching her. Christ, how long has he kept this up? Has Will noticed?

A scrappy black and white dog scurries down from upstairs and follows her to the hearth.

"Is that Reuben's dog?" Isaac demands, sliding from his stool.

Flora glances over her shoulder at him as she tosses another log onto the fire. "He says he can't care for him any longer. He thought Bess might like him." She folds her arms. "Don't give me that look, Isaac. It's just a dog."

"Reuben has eyes on you."

"Don't be ridiculous." She looks sideways at him. "Besides, what business of yours is it if a man has eyes on me?"

Isaac feels a fire inside him. She is testing him, he is sure. Then unsure. She and the moonshine are messing with his head.

"Reuben is dangerous," he says.

"I suspect he may say the same thing about you."

Isaac feels his legs sway beneath him. "Flora…"

She plants a hand on her hip. "Yes?"

He takes her arm, squeezes. Realises he is using it to stay upright. He feels a stray strand of her hair tickle his cheek. "Just be careful. I couldn't bear to see anything happen to you."

She pulls her eyes away.

He tilts his cup towards her. "May I have another?"

She takes it from him, a firm hand on his arm easing him away from her. "You've had enough, Isaac." Her voice is clipped. "Go home and see your wife."

THIEVES AND LIARS

When Scarlett wakes, Mrs Acton's house is quiet. After her sparring with the riding officer, she had crept in through the servants' entrance and stolen an apple from the kitchen to calm her raging stomach. This morning she must leave. Her ruse, she is sure, has been shattered beyond recognition.

She slides from the bed and dresses soundlessly, giving a final, longing glance to the palatial bed. When in her life will she ever sleep on something so luxurious again? Tonight she will probably be cowering beneath a bridge, fairy-led on that great expanse of moorland.

Her boots and stockings are still damp from her venture into the cave and the smell of sea hangs about her. Her coin pouch is empty.

She creeps downstairs. She can hear movement in the kitchen; the clatter of pots, two women murmuring. She smells the fire and the salty tang of fish.

She hurries away from the kitchen, tiptoeing down a long hallway. Three doors on either side. Silence behind each one.

She slips inside the first room. A bookshelf lines one wall; a great oak desk against another. She pulls back the dusty roll-top. It squeaks and sticks from disuse. A nib pen rests in a pot of dried ink. Beside it sit a gutted candle and a silver letter opener that may be worth a few shillings.

She keeps looking. The top drawer of the desk holds an array of documents and faded letters. In the second, a jar of black ink and pounce pot sit beside an embroidered handkerchief.

The third drawer rattles as it opens. The coins are loose at the bottom. Scarlett counts four pounds. Far more than she has ever had in her hand before.

She takes the handkerchief and wraps the coins carefully. Looks away as she slips the package inside her stays. She can't watch herself become a thief.

How she had scorned Isaac when she had caught him with Reuben's stolen tea. But desperation, she sees now, is a powerful motivator. How easy it is to cross that line from noble free trader to common thief. And what, really, can be expected of either of them? She knows now who their father is. She and Isaac both have a criminal's blood in them. What choice do they have but to follow in his path?

She hurries from the house. The coins make a faint bulge in her bodice, slightly below her collarbone. She covers it with her shawl.

At the top of the hill, the town stretches out before her, awakening in the grey dawn. Boats slide soundlessly from the harbour. Scarlett presses a hand over the coins. Enough to leave this place. Enough to go anywhere she desires.

But she can't leave. Not yet.

She needs to see that cottage again. She knows, of course, it is not abandoned. And she needs her father to know that she knows.

She approaches the house from the back, not daring to knock on the door. She peers tentatively through the window. This time, in the pale daylight, she can make out a table and chair, a cooking pot hanging over the hearth. The house is still. Perhaps her father had left at dawn on one of the fishing boats she had watched from the hill. Or perhaps he has been out all night, filling that cave with contraband.

She rattles the window. Locked. She grabs a rock and flings it through the glass. Unlatches the window and swings her legs over the sill.

The cottage smells of tallow and wood smoke. An empty bowl sits on the table, streaked with the hardened remains of porridge. On the shelf above the hearth is a half-burned candle in a simple brass holder. Beside it sits a jar of rust-coloured dust Scarlett assumes to be witch-powder. A similar jar had sat above the fireplace when she was a child; an ineffective plea to keep ill-luck away from her family.

This is the cottage of a poor man. Her father had not found Henry Avery's haul.

Her father is alive.

The smoke rising from the log in the grate burns away any doubt.

Scarlett drops to the floor and hugs her knees. Tears escape down her cheeks.

She had grown up thinking her father a hero. A brave adventurer who had died fighting the sea.

But Jacob Bailey is a living, breathing coward who had lied and betrayed and killed. Who had abandoned his family in the face of his debt.

Scarlett thinks of her mother. It had taken her months to accept that Jacob would not be coming home. Half a year had passed before she had requested a memorial stone be placed in the churchyard.

The sickness had fallen over her as though she had willed it. Scarlett watched as her pink cheeks yellowed, her black hair turned grey and the lively brown eyes became cloudy and distant. Her mother had always fought back against all life had thrown at her, but with her husband gone, her will to recover had disappeared. Less than a month after standing at the memorial stone and praying for her father's lost remains, Scarlett had watched her mother's coffin be lowered into the ground.

Her anger flares. She flings the bowl from the table. Snatches at the jar of witch-powder and hurls it across the hut. It smashes and spills against the flagstones. The Wild flares inside her; more bitter and angry than she has ever felt. She watches herself overturn the table, hears herself screech, feels shards of glass against her cheek as she hurls a tin cup through the window.

How can this be her father? This bastard a man who has saddled his own children with his unpayable debts? Abandoned his wife to poverty and grief.

She wants him to be dead. Fish-eaten dust at the bottom of the sea. Wants him to be nothing but a string of tainted childhood memories.

Exhaustion overtakes her. She closes her eyes and breathes deeply, sitting among the shattered pieces of her father's new life. She cannot find calm, but the urge to destroy the house has begun to fade.

She waits, letting the day slip away. She knows she needs to find a bed for the night, but she cannot leave without her father seeing her.

She paces in front of the cottage with her arms wrapped around herself. The waiting helps her adjust to the new reality. Her father the hero is dead. In his place, her father the killer, the deceiver, the liar. This new reality makes far more sense. She is not the daughter of a hero, she thinks, running a hand over the stolen coins pressed against her ribs.

In the late afternoon she sees him. He walks the overgrown path towards the cottage, hands dug into his pockets and shoulders hunched. The hair poking beneath his knitted cap has greyed and thinned, his face become leathery with sea air. But this is the man who had carried her on his shoulders and told her bedtime stories of Henry Avery's treasure. The man who had built castles with her on the beach at Talland Bay.

She walks slowly towards him, heart racing, unsure what she will do. Fury wells inside her, blurring the edges of her vision. Her mouth is dry; the tirade she had spent hours rehearsing suddenly forgotten. She wills him to speak. He stands before her on the path, the blackberry bush knocking against him as the wind skims through it.

Finally, Scarlett says: "How could you leave us?"

Jacob pauses. Frowns. There is a hardness in his eyes she does not remember. "I'm sorry, maid," he says, "whoever you think I am, you're mistaken."

Something tightens around her lungs. She feels a sudden flicker of doubt. Has her feverish search led her to the wrong man? Has she destroyed the house of a stranger? No. These eyes, these hands, that voice; they are all there in her memories. All there in pieces.

She had been a girl of five when last he had seen her. But she is his daughter. She had assumed that would be enough for him to know her in a crowd. She has her mother's face, Isaac had told her. And she has her brother's eyes, her brother's dark hair. Jacob's own rage simmering within her. The thought of not being known to him had never entered her mind. She swallows the tears in her throat.

"Asher Hales brought me here," she says finally, pinning her eyes on him so he might not turn away. "Perhaps you knew him by another name. But you'll remember him, I'm sure. You left him alone on the beach with a murdered man."

She watches Jacob's face for any reaction, any glimmer of recognition.

"I'm sorry," he says again, his colourless lips twisting into a faint smile of pity. "You have the wrong man."

THE MAN IN BLUE AND BRASS

Her father does not enter his cottage. Perhaps he sees the broken windows and the upturned table. Perhaps he wants to get as far away from Scarlett as possible.

He turns and walks back the way he came, not giving her another look.

She feels a sharp pain in her throat. Of all the scenarios she had imagined, this had not been one of them. She forces her tears away. She will not cry for this man. Will not cry for her false memories of him, for his lonely, miserable life.

But she finds herself following him. Back down the hill towards the water. She watches him enter the harbour tavern.

This place is the hideout of smugglers and illegal impressers. How can she be surprised to find him here, shoulder-to-shoulder with men she had been warned away from? Perhaps the riding officer had meant to warn her away from Jacob Bailey. He would have been right to do it.

She peers through the window of the tavern. Jacob slides a coin across the counter and carries a tankard of ale into the back room. He disappears from sight.

Scarlett makes her way around the side of the building, searching for another window so she might peer into the room. Catch sight of the men who inhabit her father's life now.

She looks through the glass. Why? Is she seeking to vindicate him? Find men clustered and plotting, her father not among them?

No. It's far too late for that. She is not trying to vindicate him, she realises. She is trying to condemn him. She wants to peer through the window to that cluster of men and see Jacob in the centre with the king's shilling in his hand. See him march from the tavern with a drugged and beaten man tossed over his shoulder, ready to be thrown onto a naval ship. She wants to pile up the black marks against his name, so she might feel no guilt when she leaves this place and pretends him dead. Feel no guilt when she kicks at that hollow farce of a memorial stone.

She feels a hand around the top of her arm. Whirls around to find the young riding officer. "Don't touch me," she hisses.

He lets his hand fall. "I told you to stay away. The men in this place are dangerous."

"I've spent my life around dangerous men. And it's taught me none of them can be trusted. Especially not those of you in blue and brass."

His eyes are close to hers. "Do you wish I arrest you, Miss Bailey?"

"Arrest me?" she snaps. "For what? I didn't bring in those goods you hid on the beach. I didn't sell them. The only thing you saw me do was pick up a packet of tobacco."

"And put it in your cloak," he reminds her. "That's enough to arrest you for theft."

She narrows her eyes. "You're a bastard."

"Of course I am. I'm paid a pittance to fight a war I've no chance of winning."

"You're a fool to have involved yourself in such a thing. Every man in this county has his hands in free trade."

"That doesn't make it right."

She snorts.

"Just go," he tells her, the hard edge disappearing from his voice. "Please. I don't want to see anything happen to you."

His sudden kindness brings fresh tears to her eyes. She blinks them away hurriedly and begins to walk from the tavern. Mrs Acton's coins slide about inside her stays. They will buy her a bed for the night, but she is too scared of being discovered a thief. If she is to buy herself a bed, it cannot be here in Portreath.

She glances up at the hills behind the village. Dusk has fallen, turning them deep purple with shadow. Dangerous and otherworldly, alive with spirits. They stretch into the night and seem to go on forever.

"Where are you going?" the officer asks.

"It's none of your business." She feels her tears threatening.

"Do you have somewhere to go? A bed for the night?"

"Of course I have a bed," she says, trying for sharpness but managing no more than a choked whisper. Wind tunnels in from the sea and tugs at her skirts.

"Is there someone here for you?" he asks. "A friend? Family?"

At the thought of family, Scarlett's tears spill. She longs suddenly for that cottage on the hill in Talland. Longs for the way it had been before she had proclaimed her brother a thief and a liar. She longs to sit around the table eating Caroline's flavourless broth, stirring up Isaac and listening to a stream of Gabriel's jabber. She longs for the time when Jacob Bailey had been a memory.

She swipes hurriedly at her tears.

"Come with me," the officer says gently.

Scarlett hesitates. This man has sworn an oath to cleanse the country of free trade. He had watched her slide smuggled tobacco into her cloak. But the night is thickening, and the hills are crawling with spirits. If anyone from Mrs Acton's household sees her, they will string her up for theft.

There is little to do but follow him.

They wind through the streets towards a cluster of crooked stone houses. Some are leaning so sharply they seem to be holding each other up. The officer stops at the cottage on the corner.

"This is your house?" Scarlett asks throatily.

He nods. "In part, at least. I rent the room at the back." He leads her down the side of the building to a small door at the rear. "It's not much. But you're cold. And there's a fire. A kettle."

Scarlett wrings her cloak around her hands.

"You don't trust me," he says.

"Can you blame me?"

"I suppose not." He slides a key from his pocket and unlocks the door. "Do as you wish." He steps inside. The house is small and cramped, the single room cluttered with a table and two chairs. A narrow bed sits against one wall. The place smells faintly of musk soap.

Scarlett stays planted in the doorway. "I don't even know your name."

He looks over his shoulder at her. "It's Jamie. Jamie McCulley." He goes to the hearth and tosses a handful of kindling into the grate. Strikes the tinderbox.

Scarlett closes her eyes. She doesn't want to be this bitter, untrusting person. She wants her old optimism. Wants the sun that shone over everything until Asher Hales and his cursed letter had barrelled into her life.

She steps inside the cottage.

Is this her most foolish act of all? Walking willingly into the home of a riding officer?

Jamie looks up from the hearth where a tiny flame has begun to lick the wood. "Close the door. That wind's got a right chill to it."

The door closes with a heavy click. Scarlett looks about her. Despite its size, the house is clean and tidy, pots stacked neatly on a shelf beside jars of oatmeal and potted meat. A blue and gold riding officer's jacket hangs on a hook beside the door.

Scarlett swallows heavily. She looks back at Jamie, trying to see behind his eyes. Can she trust this decency? He has already trapped her once.

He unwinds his scarf and slides off his coat. Holds out a hand. "Your cloak?"

Scarlett shakes her head. She cannot stay long. Cannot make herself comfortable here in the home of a revenue man. A mouthful of tea to warm her and then she will be gone.

Jamie hangs the kettle on the hook above the fire. He goes to the shelf and returns with bread and cheese. Breaks a piece from the loaf and hands it to Scarlett. She kneels by the hearth, holding her frozen fingers close to the flames.

She chews slowly. The events of the day have stolen her appetite, but she had best force down a few mouthfuls if she is going to make it out of Portreath tonight.

In her mind's eye, she sees the blank look in her father's eyes.

You have the wrong man.

She blinks hard, trying to force him from her thoughts. She hates how much their meeting has rattled her.

The stool squeaks behind her. Jamie cuts a piece of cheese and pops it into his mouth. He holds the knife out to her. She shakes her head. Her eyes fix on the small leather-bound book on the shelf beside the food jars. She has heard the riding officers keep journals of their exploits. Has Jamie kept his own records of seized liquor and chases in the night? He catches her looking and she pulls her eyes away hurriedly.

"Why smuggling?" he asks.

Why smuggling? She has never been asked such a thing. Why smuggling? Why air? Why sleep? There has never been any other option.

"It's all I know," she mumbles, not looking at him. The shame of it hits her hard. She had grown up believing the words spouted by her father and the other men in the village. Smuggling was the noblest of trades. A trade that brought power back to the people. But with Jamie's eyes on her, the life she has built does not seem quite so noble.

Smuggling and theft. All she knows.

A thin line of steam begins to rise from the kettle. Jamie pours the tea into two mugs and hands one to her. She wraps her hands around it, feeling heat seep through the tin. "My father was a smuggler," she says. "I had little choice but to follow his path."

"Your father is dead?"

She stares into her mug. "Ayes," she says finally. "My father is dead." She hears her voice waver. What is this? Is she to mourn the man all over again? Why should she feel sad? This is the way it has always been.

My father is dead has not elicited grief from her for many years. Yet now her chest is aching and her tears are threatening to return.

She takes a gulp of tea.

"Why were you alone at the tavern tonight?" she asks, desperate to change the subject. "Riding officers don't work alone. And they don't spend their nights lurking about in ale houses."

Jamie doesn't speak at once. "Unofficial business," he says after a moment.

"The press gang."

He nods.

"How do you hope to stop them? A riding officer has no power over the navy."

"The gang is operating illegally," says Jamie. "They're thugs hired by the magistrate and are working without a press warrant. They're taking the money intended for the impressed sailors and keeping it for themselves. The navy has little involvement before they ship the poor bastards off to war."

"How do you know all this?"

"Speculation," he admits. "My brother was one of the men taken. I'm sure of it. He disappeared from the harbour tavern several months ago."

Scarlett's eyes meet his in a moment of sympathy. But she says: "How do you know your brother did not just stumble drunkenly into the sea?"

Jamie flinches slightly and Scarlett regrets her words.

"My brother worked for the revenue service like me," he tells her. "He long suspected the traders on this coast were involved in more than smuggling. He witnessed a rendezvous between the naval officers and the magistrate. Saw the magistrate speaking with the men we suspect are smugglers on more than one occasion."

"You think your local magistrate is crooked?"

He gives a humourless laugh. "My colleagues and I have brought five men before the court for smuggling this year. Each has had their case thrown out. We've begun taking men to trial in Saint Ives."

Scarlett realises she is staring. She stands abruptly. Jamie's words have reminded her that they are ingrained on opposite sides of the law. "I wish you luck," she says.

He frowns. "Where are you going?"

"I need to get home to Talland."

"You're leaving tonight? How? There's no coach out of here for three days."

"I'll walk," she says, pushing aside thoughts of the black-ink hills. She will walk those hills and slide past the spirits and go back to being that woman who is not afraid of the dark.

"It's many days' walk," says Jamie. "You'll get home far quicker if you wait for the coach."

"I need to leave now."

"What's the urgency?"

But of course, she can tell him nothing of the urgency. Not of the stolen coins inside her bodice, or the man on his way to Talland to turn her family in for smuggling.

Instead, she admits: "I've nowhere to sleep." Her shoulders sink.

Jamie stands, reaching for his uniform. "You'll sleep here. I've a watch tonight. I'll be out until early morning. I can sleep a few hours at the customs station when I return."

"No," Scarlett says instinctively. "I couldn't."

He wraps a faded blue scarf around his neck. "Trust me or don't. The choice is yours. But the place will be empty and it'll be far warmer here than out on those hills." He buttons the coat and nods towards the cheese sitting on the table. "Finish it if you wish."

Scarlett glances out the window at the thick dark. Looks back at the fire and the bed. She draws in her breath and manages a faint nod. "I'll be out by dawn."

MEN OF WAR

Isaac borrows a wagon from the Millers' farm to make
the delivery. He waits until the Mariner's Arms has closed
for the night before climbing into the tunnel with John Baker
and Will Francis. They carry out the ankers and load them
into the wagon, hiding the goods beneath a layer of kelp.
And up through the dark they go, following the ribbon of a
road towards Lansallos.

The cliffs above the cove are blue-black and bare. Below
them, the beach is empty. Isaac is jittery with anticipation.
He had told Caroline of the sale. Seen her excitement.
Enough for two tickets, he had told her. A ticket out of
Reuben's life for each of their children.

They wait in the dark, the lantern circling in the wind and
making shadows pitch. An invisible sea sighs in the cove.

"You sure he's a good thing?" Baker asks. "This
innkeeper?"

Isaac turns up the collar of his coat against the cold. "He
wants a cheap sale." But there is a discomfort in him he is

unable to shake. This new immorality makes him feel alive, but it also makes him wary. He slides a hand into his pocket, feeling the cold metal of his pistol. He cocks and uncocks the trigger.

Light moves across the clifftops. A second wagon clatters towards them.

"Thought you weren't going to show," Isaac tells the innkeeper with a crooked smile.

The man chuckles. "Pound an anker? Course I'm going to show."

Isaac climbs from the wagon and pulls aside the kelp. He and the men load the brandy into the innkeeper's cart.

"Twenty pounds," he says, once the ankers are loaded.

The innkeeper hands him the money. "Why such a good price?"

Isaac squeezes the coins between his fingers. A ticket for Gabriel. A ticket for Mary. "I'm paying you to keep your mouth shut. Not a word to Tom Leach about who sold you this brandy."

The innkeeper doesn't return his smile. "It weren't me who said a word," he says. "But perhaps Leach already knows."

"Why do you say that?"

"He came to the inn the very same evening as you. Brandy for sale, he said. I told him I weren't interested."

Isaac curses under his breath. Had Leach followed him to the Well House? "Did you tell him you already had a sale?"

"Didn't say a thing. Like I told you. But the man's no fool."

No fool indeed. Isaac is the one who had behaved rashly; scrabbling for a sale with Leach breathing down his neck. His stomach clenches.

He watches the innkeeper climb back into the wagon and disappear into the dark. He waits. Beneath the constant roar of the sea, an owl coos.

Isaac squints. Is the dark moving? His eyes strain and clutch at the shadows. He had been careful to ensure they had not been followed on the journey from Talland. But if Leach were to come to Lansallos, he would have approached from Polruan. Would have followed the innkeeper.

Isaac has sunk Leach's ship, undercut his business. And Leach is not a man who will let such things slide.

There is little to do but return to Talland.

The lantern at the front of the coach sends an arc of light swaying across the hills. It moves over the horse's slender back, picking out shapes on either side of the road.

Something moves in the light. There, to the left of the coach. A fox? Or something more? Isaac swallows, his mouth dry. He snaps the reins and the horse quickens its pace. The wagon pitches as the road spirals upwards. Beside him, Will Francis looks edgily over his shoulder.

More movement. This time, too big to be an animal. A pistol shot explodes in the blackness. It flies into the side of the wagon, wood splintering. The horse charges.

The path is narrow. Keep on at this speed and they risk pitching over the cliff edge. But nor can they slow. The men firing at them will be on horseback. They will be far quicker than the wagon.

Isaac looks over his shoulder at the dark expanse of the hills. They can lose themselves in the blackness. He touches the pistol in his pocket. The thought of firing back makes his stomach swirl.

A second bullet flies into the wheel of the wagon. Isaac stops the horse and douses the lantern, plunging them into blackness. The three men scramble out, burying themselves in the banks of furze lining the road. Another bullet flies into the night.

There is movement around him. His eyes adjusting to the dark, or his imagination? He sees the inky shape of a man, pistol trained on Will.

A shot shatters the momentary stillness. The man in the darkness falls.

Isaac realises he has his pistol out. He feels heat go through him. Is it his bullet in the man's chest? He doesn't remember firing. But his gun is hot. Empty. He hears Will breathe hard.

Isaac lies flat to the ground, feeling his heart thump against the earth. Feeling the vibration of hooves.

"Put your weapons down!"

Riding officers.

They shine their lamp through the dark. The white light illuminates the face of Tom Leach.

Leach fires. A riding officer falls from his horse. His lamp shatters on the earth and the blackness returns. A thunder of hooves as his horse charges up the hill. Has the second officer escaped? Is he waiting in the dark? Can he see which man pulled the trigger?

A second shot from Leach. The spark from the pistol lights the night. Another body falls.

From his hiding place, Isaac sees Leach slide from his horse and stand over the riding officers' bodies.

"Dead," he tells his men. "We need to leave."

"What about Bailey?"

Leach's response is inaudible. He leaps onto his horse and charges away from the lifeless men.

Isaac peers into the faint moonlight. Baker is on his knees behind the wagon. He grips his side, worms of blood trickling through his fingers.

"Christ," Isaac hisses, "can you stand?"

Baker nods. He climbs slowly to his feet, leaning heavily on Isaac. Will hurries towards them. Baker groans and curses as he stumbles into the wagon, his blood leaving dark streaks down the front of Isaac's greatcoat.

Isaac climbs into the box seat. He snaps the reins and the horse charges up the narrow path. Baker groans as they rattle through a ditch.

Isaac grits his teeth. The nearest doctor is in Plymouth, a day's ride away. Logic tells him the horse will never make it if they keep up at this speed. But it feels foolish to slow the wagon with an injured man inside. The jolting rattles his body, his thoughts. He sees the man in the darkness fall. Feels the gun hot in his hand.

Sweat prickles his forehead. A man is dead on account of him.

A man who would have killed Will had he not acted first.

There is no place in this life for morality, for sentiment. No place for a man unwilling to pull the trigger.

Will climbs into the box seat beside him. "The wound is deep. He's losing too much blood. We've got to get him help."

"We'll take him to the inn," Isaac hears himself say. "Flora can help him. Give him something for the pain at least."

What is he doing? He doesn't want Flora any deeper in her mother's craft after the way the villagers had come after her last week. But the groans from the back of the wagon are turning his stomach.

107

The lights of Talland break the horizon.

Isaac's head is still swimming when he thumps on the door of the Mariner's Arms.

"Isaac. What's happened?" Flora tugs a pale blue shawl around her. She is barefoot in her nightshift, long blonde hair spilling over her shoulders. Her eyes fall to the bloodstains splattered across his coat. "Are you hurt?"

"John Baker's been shot. I'm afraid he'll not make it to Plymouth."

A look of uncertainty passes across her eyes and Isaac regrets coming. But she says:

"Where is he?"

"In the wagon outside."

She nods towards the hearth. A log glows orange in the grate. "Stoke the fire." She runs upstairs, returning moments later with the kettle and a handful of small, dark leaves. She crushes the fronds into a cup and hangs the kettle above the fire. Her eyes are hard and determined.

"Take a little brandy," she tells Isaac. "Give it to him for the pain."

Steam begins to curl from the kettle. She pours the boiling water over the leaves.

Isaac follows her out to the wagon. John Baker's wife has been fetched and is sitting beside her husband, his bloodstained hand in hers. Soundless tears run down her cheeks. Will sits at Baker's other side, his coat pressed to the wound above his hip.

Isaac hands Will the cup of brandy. "Give him this."

Flora climbs across the blood-splattered kelp. She eases Will's hand away and lifts Baker's blackened shirt. "I need more light."

Isaac unhooks the lantern from the front of the wagon and kneels behind her, feeling the heat of the lamp against his cheek.

She pulls the leaves from the cup and lays them carefully over the wound. Baker shifts and sighs. She presses a fresh cloth to his hip, gesturing to his wife to hold it in place.

"The yarrow will slow the bleeding," she says. "But you've got to get him to a doctor as soon as possible."

Mrs Baker gives a sob of thanks.

Isaac and Flora climb from the wagon and watch as it disappears up the hill. They walk wordlessly back to the inn. Flora lets out a long breath.

"You did a fine job," Isaac says, pressing a hand to her shoulder.

Flora manages a small smile. She empties the kettle into the trough behind the bar and scrubs the blood from her hands. "Will you stay a moment?" Her eyes are pleading; voicing that loneliness he knows she would never allow herself to admit to. She pours two cups of brandy and presses one into his hand, not waiting for his response.

These are the times he feels for her the most; this time of night when the inn has closed and her daughter sleeps and the empty rooms gape around her. No, he thinks, he does not want to be alone either.

He slides off his bloodstained coat and tosses it over one of the stools. He takes a long sip, the liquor steadying him a little. Flora sits by the hearth, her shawl sliding from one shoulder. Firelight flickers on her cheek, making her pale hair shine. Isaac sits beside her, drawing his knees to his chest. When had he last seen her like this; barefoot, with hair tumbling down her back? Not since they were children, tearing across the rim of the water, the beach seeming as though it would go on forever.

She brings her cup to her lips and watches the fire. Isaac feels her eyes drift to him. "Was Leach involved?" she asks finally, her question shattering the stillness.

He takes another mouthful of brandy. Nods. "He and his men ambushed us on the way back from Lansallos."

"How did he know you were there?"

"He must have seen me at the Well House. Suspected things perhaps. Followed the innkeeper."

"One of Leach's men came to the inn the night you were in Guernsey," Flora tells him, staring into her cup. "Prying. Asking after you. I thought little of it at the time. But I ought to have told you."

Isaac touches her bare wrist.

Don't blame yourself.

Her skin is hot.

"The riding officers showed themselves," he says. "The two of them were killed."

Flora exhales sharply. "Killed by who? Leach?"

"Ayes." As he speaks of dead men, his heart begins to thunder again. A fresh wave of dizziness rips through him. He is suddenly far too hot to sit by the fire. He stands, stumbles. His empty cup clatters against the flagstones. Flora leaps to her feet and takes his arm.

"There's something else, ayes? Tell me what."

He closes his eyes. "One of Leach's men is dead. I fear it was me who shot him."

For a moment, Flora doesn't speak. The fire pops loudly.

"You shot a man who was firing at you?" she says finally. "And what were you to have done? Stand by and let him kill you?"

He opens his eyes. Shadows dance in the firelight, making everything unsteady. She presses her hands to his cheeks. "You did what you had to do," she says. "To survive. I don't know what I would have done if it had been you lying in that wagon tonight. And I don't know what I would have done if you'd gone to make that delivery and never come home."

Her hands slide from his face and grip the laces of his shirt. The spicy scent of yarrow hangs about her, tinged with soap and brandy. He can feel the heat of her body through her thin nightshift. The linen clings to the curves of her hips.

He swallows. "It's late. I ought to leave." He turns for the door, but Flora keeps her hands clenched around his collar. She tugs him back to her.

And he stops thinking. Kisses her hard. She will pull away, of course. She has not given up on goodness the way he has. But she is pushing her body against his, clutching fistfuls of his shirt. She is sighing into his mouth as his hand slides beneath her shift. She is in his hair, inside his breeches, a dizzying blur of white skin and roaming lips.

And then they are no longer standing; the fire-warmed flagstones hot beneath their bodies. She has lost her shawl. When? Isaac has no thought of it. Her narrow fingers are pulling his shirt over his head, seeking the sparse curls of hair on his chest. The flames heat his cheeks, his neck, his back. His skin is blazing.

Stop, he thinks distantly. *Stop.*

But the thought is pushed out by Flora's mouth against his. Her willingness to pull her shift to her waist. Her hot hands tug his body to hers.

He is inside her before his conscience catches him. What use is there trying for morality? He has blood on his hands now. There is no point seeking decency, so he may as well seek happiness, however fleeting and lustful, however driven by stress and brandy and men lying lifeless on the road.

He opens his eyes when he feels her still beneath him. Her hair is spilling over the flagstones like fallen snow. Their eyes meet. Where do they go from here? Do they retreat to silence, to the old pattern of friendship, to never speaking of this night again? Never speaking of it and never speaking of it and never speaking of it until it is over and forgotten and gone?

He sees shards of green in her eyes, the faint powder of freckles on her cheeks. Feels her ragged breath against his chin. He lowers himself to her, kisses her lips and the hollow curve of her throat. Her pulse vibrates against his mouth. He doesn't want this to be forgotten and gone. He wants it to have just begun.

Flora pushes him back and sits suddenly. Her eyes are wide and anxious, as though she has snapped out of a spell and caught sight of what they have done.

Isaac reaches for his shirt. "I'm sorry. I'll leave. I—"

She clamps a hand over his, stilling him.

"Riding officers were killed," she says. "A man in blue staring at the sky." She hugs her knees. "I saw it in my mother's mirror."

"That's impossible," Isaac says, without thinking. *That's impossible* is an instinctive reaction to years of Scarlett's ghost stories. He regrets saying it to Flora. He pushes her hair aside and holds his lips to her neck. "You don't believe in such things. You never have."

She says: "I'm not sure that's true."

"Of course it's true. You've always had a rational mind."

Why is he so eager for her to be wrong? Why such desperation for a solid, unbending world?

He needs the reliability of it, Isaac realises. He can't have the solidity of his world upturned by images in a black mirror. His life is shifting around him. He is watched by a man who will kill him if he discovers his deception, is flooded with desire for a woman who is not his wife. His sister has vanished, and he will tear across the world in search of a new home. Take rationality out of his life and he fears he may drown.

STORY-TELLERS

Three days until Asher is paid. Three days until he escapes this filthy, menial job of mucking out another man's stables.

For four days, he has barely ventured from the farm in case he crosses paths with Jacob or Scarlett. The week has been a mindless blur of shovelling, hauling and hoeing. The place has left him with the incessant feeling of bugs crawling beneath his skin. There is a chill inside him he fears he will never warm from.

He longs to wash, to shave, to change his clothes. Three days, he tells himself. Three days and he will be free. Three days and he will be on the road to the Polperro customs house. Out will come his tales of false-bottomed luggers and smuggling tunnels.

Forgive me, Callie, I loved you once.

It is late afternoon. He carries the sack of feed to the stables for the horses. An hour or two before the work day is done. He will eat gruel. Sleep. Spend a few blissful hours lost in his dreams.

They come for him before his mind can make sense of it. The sack is knocked from his arms, grain spilling. He flails, trying to reach the shovel. The hands around his arms are vice-like, his feet almost lifted from the ground. His head is held, something pungent and vicious poured down his throat. He coughs, splutters. Hands are clamped over his mouth and nose, forcing him to swallow. The world blurs and there is dark.

The lugger lurches back towards Polperro harbour, deck shimmering with baskets of pilchards. Isaac blinks hard, grateful for the sudden wall of spray that flies over the gunwale, washing away his exhaustion.

He had stumbled back to the cottage long after midnight with Baker's blood on his greatcoat and Flora's scent on his hands. Had slept would could barely have been an hour before dawn had pushed through the windows and he'd stumbled in a daze to the fishing port.

He rubs his eyes and watches from the foredeck as the village grows larger.

The harbour is busy. People are milling about by the water's edge, restless as bugs in a jar. This is the way of this village, Isaac knows. When shots are fired, or ghosts walk the hills, the people flock together and work themselves into nightmares, seeking out answers from whichever poor soul they feel can provide them. The vicar, the healer, the leader of the smuggling ring.

For all their midnight landings and whispered plots, Isaac knows his role in the syndicate is a poorly kept secret.

He had said nothing about the previous night to the fishing crew. Played down the absence of both John Baker and Will Francis.

An illness, yes. Spreading? Most likely.

Deadly?

In his mind, he heard Baker groan as his blood stained kelp and straw. Had he survived the wagon ride to Plymouth? Survived the barber surgeon's bullet extractor? Isaac knows it unlikely.

He looks back towards the harbour. No doubt the riding officers' bodies have been found. An investigation has begun. The villagers will have questions, Isaac is sure. And they will come to him.

But he must remain silent. Ignorant. He must walk through that crowd with his head down. No one can know the real reason for John Baker's absence. No one can know he and Isaac were riding the roads of Lansallos last night.

Not Reuben, not the authorities.

There will be dragoons at the cottage door later, Isaac is sure. Trailed by wolf-eyed riding officers, keen for a rare conviction. Rival smuggling gangs suspected. Isaac knows the revenue service believes him involved in free trade. They'd have him condemned if it weren't for lack of proof. He had best keep his story short and straight.

Children pour from the charity school in a flurry of giggles and chatter. Flora peers through the chaos of blue smocks and bonnets for her daughter. She wills Bessie to hurry.

She had gone about her day as though nothing had happened. Comb and pin her hair and pretend she had not tended to Baker's gunshot wound. Make porridge and pretend she had not asked Isaac to stay. Walk Bessie to school and pretend she had not seen the conflict in her mirror.

She feels eyes on her as she waits by the church. The maid from the vicarage walks past on her way to the market. Two fishermen eye her as they stride towards the cliff path. She sees Caroline on the other side of the street, waiting for her son. Flora turns away hurriedly. It feels as if they know it all.

Witch. Charlatan.
Adulterer.

In a moment of brandy and firelight, her conscience had left her. She has always prided herself on her strength, but with Isaac's breath on her skin, she'd abandoned her resolve. She has become one of those whispering, red-faced women who had appeared so regularly at her mother's door. Shilling for a course of Queen Anne's Lace to prevent an unwanted child. Flora's skin burns at the thought; a heady mix of desire and shame.

Bessie shrieks with laughter as she flies out of the gate with one of her friends. Her cheeks are flushed, her blonde hair a spidery mess, escaping out the sides of her bonnet. Barely a trace of her illness left, Flora thinks. Her mind is a tangle. Healing stones and yarrow leaves, magic mirrors and the allure of a married man.

Bessie's hand in hers, she hurries towards the cliff path. A crowd has gathered at the harbour; villagers chattering nervously by the water's edge. She sees Isaac's lugger sliding towards the docks. And there is Charles Reuben striding down the hill towards the commotion.

No doubt word of the murders has spread. Flora quickens her pace. She wants the silent safety of her inn.

Before she reaches the cliff path, she hears the rap of hooves behind her. Hears: "Good afternoon, Mrs Kelly."

She curses under her breath. "Go on ahead," she tells Bessie. "Wait for me at the top of the hill."

She turns reluctantly. The two riding officers are familiar. One old, one young. Polished buttons, polished boots. Shorn chins and red noses. They had been drinking at the Mariner's Arms the night Isaac had been to Guernsey.

"Good afternoon," Flora says stiffly.

The men swing themselves from their horses. Boots thud dully on the earth.

"How is business?" the older officer asks.

"Fine, thank you very much." Flora eyes the crowd. Caroline and her children are making their way towards the harbour. The fishing boats knock against their moorings. Women from the pilchard palace elbow their way through the crowd, trying to retrieve the baskets from the decks of the lugger.

"Two riding officers were killed close to Lansallos Cove last night," the officer tells Flora. "We assume the shootings were the work of a smuggling gang."

"I see. How dreadful." She grits her teeth. Deflects their questions.

Who was at your tavern last night?
Did you see anything unusual?
Has there been any trouble of late?

"There's been no trouble," she says shortly.

"I hope you'll be watchful. Violence among trading gangs is becoming increasingly common. This is not a good time for a woman to be running a business alone."

She gives a wry smile. "Then I suppose I ought to close my doors until I find myself a husband."

The officer pushes past her iciness. "Perhaps you've heard talk among the men who frequent your tavern. Heard of plans, perhaps, or rivalries."

A clamour of voices floats up from the harbour. "I'm sure the men involved in this conflict have far more sense than to let their plans be overheard by the innkeeper."

The officer tugs at his reins as the horse shifts restlessly. He meets Flora's eyes in an attempt at camaraderie. "If you're afraid of speaking out against these men, we can offer you protection. It is of utmost importance that an arrest is made over these murders. The smugglers involved need to be made an example of, in order to put an end to this rising violence."

She gives a short smile. "I don't need protection against the smugglers. Thank you."

The officer considers her a moment. He swaps a glance with his colleague. Lowers his voice. "We can also offer protection against the excisemen." He looks at her pointedly. "Should you require it."

Flora swallows heavily. Protection from the excisemen is an alluring prospect. Protection against the forged licence on her wall. But all she knows of the conflict she had learned from Isaac. She cannot give the officers information without revealing her sources. "I don't need protection from the excisemen either," she says, forcing a smile. "I have nothing to hide."

Isaac strides through the crowd with his head down, ignoring the questions being flung at him from every side.

What do you know?

What did you see?

Caroline shivers. It unnerves her how quickly gossip spreads in this place.

"A word, Mr Bailey?" Isaac looks up at the sound of Reuben's voice.

Caroline hands the baby to Gabriel and ushers him off to play on the beach. She elbows her way towards the two men. Up close, she sees shadows of sleeplessness on Isaac's cheeks. Sees that flicker behind his eyes that warns her his patience is thin. He glances sideways at her.

"Mrs Bailey," Reuben says smoothly, "you needn't bother yourself with our business."

"My husband's business is my business."

Reuben looks at Isaac, who nods for him to begin. She is glad he has not dismissed her.

"You've heard of the conflict in Lansallos, I assume?" Reuben says finally. "Two riding officers were murdered." His gaze is firmly fixed on Isaac, as though Caroline weren't there.

"I've heard."

"The authorities assume a conflict between rival trading gangs."

Isaac says nothing. He had been tight-lipped with her too, Caroline thinks. Had told her only the bare outline of the story. The riding officers killed by Tom Leach as they intercepted the conflict between the two gangs. John Baker shot. She wonders what details Isaac had left out. Wonders if he would have said anything at all had she not been waiting by the fire when he walked into the cottage carrying a blood-splattered greatcoat.

"Do you know anything of it?" asks Reuben.

"Why would I know anything of it?" Isaac says brusquely.

"You and your men will be suspects. Customs already have their eyes on you."

Caroline sees Isaac's jaw tense. She wills him to keep calm. Anger will not convince Reuben of his innocence. Nor will it convince the revenue men.

"I had nothing to do with what happened last night," he says. "I was at home with my family."

Reuben's eyes shift, as though trying to determine if he is telling the truth. Caroline feels something turn over in her stomach.

"What business would the men and I have had in Lansallos? Our next run isn't for a month."

"No," Reuben says. "It's not." He makes a noise in his throat. Weighted silence hangs between them. An old woman pushes through the crowd towards Isaac, then darts away as she catches sight of Reuben.

"Why are you still here?" Isaac snaps. "I've told you I know nothing."

"I'm still here," Reuben says tersely, "because I'm not sure I believe you."

He snorts. "Fourteen years of loyalty and this is how you repay me? They're saying two riding officers were shot at close range. Do you truly think me capable of such a thing?"

Reuben stands close. The creases in his face are deep. He is growing old. He has no heir, Caroline thinks distantly. If he were to die, her family would be free.

"I'm not entirely sure what you're capable of," he tells Isaac. "I don't know how much of your father is in you."

"What exactly does that mean?" Isaac turns to leave, but Reuben clamps a firm hand over his forearm, preventing him from leaving. Isaac yanks his arm free. "You've no power, Reuben. Without Bobby Carter's protection you'll answer to the law like the rest of us. What will you do? Shoot me? Risk hanging for murder?"

Caroline grits her teeth. She tries to catch his eye. *Stop.*

Reuben's cheeks redden with anger. "You're a fool to be so brash, Bailey. You're a man with much to lose."

"Go to hell," Isaac spits. He turns abruptly and marches towards the path back to Talland. Caroline calls hurriedly for Gabriel and chases her husband up onto the cliffs.

She is breathless by the time she reaches him. Wind tears at their hair and clothing, sends bracken and blackberry bushes bending towards the sea. She wants to lace her fingers through his and tell him to be calm. She wants to take his arm, smooth his hair, kiss his cheek. But she does none of these things.

Half way home, Isaac says: "Do you think he knows?" He doesn't look at her.

Caroline doesn't answer at once. She quickens her pace to walk beside him. "Perhaps." The response feels stupid, but it is all she can think of to say. She is glad Isaac has not shut her out. "Is there anything you might have done to make him suspicious?"

He shakes his head slightly. "We were careful. Discreet."

"Yes, well, somehow Tom Leach found out you were in Lansallos. It's possible Reuben did too." She wonders again what had happened on those cliffs. There are things her husband is keeping from her, of that she is sure. But she knows better than to hound him while there is fire behind his eyes. Instead, she says: "you said we had enough for two tickets."

Leaving Talland has never been more pressing. With Reuben on one side and Asher Hales and his secrets on the other, Caroline is sure she will crumble unless they escape this place soon.

"Two tickets, ayes," Isaac says finally. "But selling the rest of the brandy will be difficult. The riding officers will be all over the area. And I can't sell to the Well House. Leach obviously knows I've been dealing with the innkeeper."

"Then you need to find another buyer. Perhaps head east? Away from Leach."

"It will take time. We need to be patient."

"We don't have the luxury of patience," Caroline snaps, her own anxiety tearing free.

"We can't start behaving rashly at the first hint of trouble." Isaac doesn't look at her. He says again: "We need to be patient."

And here are the doubts Caroline has been refusing to let take hold. Doubts she can no longer ignore. For all Isaac's talk of breaking free of Reuben, there is something holding him to Talland, something stealing his urgency and dampening his desire for escape.

Scarlett perhaps. Yes, Caroline understands. She doesn't like it, but she understands. When they leave this place, they will tell no one where they are going. Will never speak of it aloud in case Reuben's men are listening. Talland will be a place they can never return to. And if they leave before Scarlett comes home, she knows Isaac and his sister might never be reunited.

IMPRESSMENT

Scarlett curls up on her bed in her boots and cloak and lets her eyes drift closed. She had left Jamie's cottage at dawn, determined to be gone before he returned from his watch. She had pushed her trust for him far enough. Best now that they forget each other.

In the rising sun she had walked out of Portreath, following the road the coach had taken. There were villages this way, she remembered. Villages filled with dust covered miners who spent their days digging treasures from the hills. Follow the road, she told herself, as the clouds closed in over the sun. Follow the road and the spirits in the hills would not lead her astray.

She had reached Redruth by mid-morning and found an inn on the edge of the village.

A bed for two nights. She slid the stolen coins across the counter, keeping her eyes as blank and innocent as when she encountered riding officers while running goods up Talland Hill.

And so, a bed. A small victory. In two days, the coach will leave for the south coast and she can go back to believing her father is gone. She runs a finger absentmindedly over the coins. Where else could they take her? What else might she see? She thinks of the colourful world of Isaac's travel stories. Thinks of palaces and mountains and men speaking in other tongues. She tries to imagine herself immersed in such a world. She can't do it, she realises. Isaac's stories are all she has to build the image on. She cannot imagine mountains or palaces. Can't see herself immersed in anything but free trade.

She kicks off her boots and lies back on the bed. Orange light is pushing through the curtains, the night drawing nearer. Another woman enters the room, clutching a faded saddle bag to her chest. She goes to the bed beside Scarlett's and takes off her cloak. Scarlett checks her shawl is covering the bulge of the coins.

Jamie McCulley is in her head.

Jamie who had made her tea and slept on a chair at the customs house so she might have a safe night's rest.

No, these thoughts are dangerous. He has brass buttons and a riding officer's journal and friends in high places.

Jamie who had led her into the cave and set her up for smuggling. Neat, preachy, *that doesn't make it right* Jamie.

Good. This is safer.

But what does it matter? She has left Portreath. When the carriage comes it will take her further and further from that tidy little room at the back of the stone cottage.

Where is he, she wonders? What is he doing? Is he prowling the harbour tavern, searching for the hideout of the press gang? Galloping along the clifftops in a flurry of blue and gold?

And are there men in that tavern by the cliffs tossing back tainted liquor, unaware they are about to be hauled off to war?

Scarlett's mind goes to a man in a white wig, pushing a glass of scented brandy into her hand. *Armagnac*, he had told her. But she knows the smell of Armagnac. And it was not what had been in the glass.

Is the man in the wig one of the impressers?

He had trailed and touched and crooned over her. If she were to bend to his advances, could she pull information from him? Could she catch the press gang mid-operation as Jamie has been unable to do?

No. Such a thing is dangerous. Foolish. This is someone else's battle. Besides, she has already left Portreath.

She thinks of Jamie and his vanished brother. Thinks of his hot eyes as he had told her of his desire to catch out the impressers. She sits abruptly. Someone else's battle, yes, but she does not want him to fight it alone.

The other woman peers at her from over the washstand. Scarlett pulls on her boots and cloak and leaves the inn before she changes her mind.

The light is draining quickly. She walks fast, eyes on the path. Follow the road and she will be safe. She will not be fairy-led by the spirits haunting these hills.

The sky is icy pink beneath the clouds. The engine house of the mine is silhouetted on a distant hill. She crosses a peak and the sea unfolds below her. Portreath is close. She winds her way down into the village, wind lashing her hair against her cheeks. Gulls swoop and screech, then are carried back towards the clouds on a sudden updraught of air.

Scarlett hurries towards the tavern. In the early evening, the place is quiet. Peering through the window, she sees the innkeeper leaning on the bar. He is chatting to a fisherman in an enormous tarred coat. No sign of the man in the wig.

No sign of Jacob.

Ought she wait for wigged man to appear? There is no guarantee, of course, that he will come tonight.

She needs to explore the tavern. How are the impressers taking the drugged men to the navy? What is Jamie missing?

Never mind that the man with the wig is not here. There are other men inside she can get close to. Other men she can persuade to tell her their secrets.

She takes off her shortgown and crams it into her pocket. She unpins her hair, letting it spill over her shoulders in sea-hardened waves. Tightens the laces of her bodice and tugs her stomacher low.

She prays her father is not inside to see her.

What does it matter? Her father has no idea who she is.

Blood thumping, she shoves her way inside the tavern. The front room is busy, noisy. Heads turn as she enters. The innkeeper catches her eye and beckons with a grimy finger.

"You best watch yourself, maid," he says as she draws closer. "If you're looking for the traders again, now's not the time to do it." He nods towards two uniformed men drinking in the corner. "Customs are paying us a visit."

"I'm not here for the traders," she says brusquely. "Like you said, there are other ways a girl can earn a few shillings." She tries to force away the colour she feels rising in her cheeks. She is doing this for Jamie, she tells herself.

The innkeeper chuckles, eying the swell of her breasts at the top of her stays. "Indeed there are." He leans over the bar. "I have money."

Scarlett shakes off her revulsion. "You also got a tavern to run."

He grins. "Perhaps you come back for me later."

She flashes him a sickly smile and makes her way into the back room. It is darker here. Colder. A few men sit at the tables, glasses in front of them and pipes in their hands. A curtain of smoke hangs over them. Their conversation is low, punctuated by bursts of gravelly laughter.

She feels eyes on her. Her mouth is suddenly dry. She edges hesitantly towards one of the tables. Before she reaches it, she hears a voice close to her ear.

"Not seen you in here before."

The man is barely taller than her. His cheeks are pink, stomach straining against the buttons of his worn blue waistcoat. His grey streaked hair is tied back messily. He stands close to her, swaying slightly.

Scarlett forces a smile. "You got money?"

"Of course."

"Good." She glances around the room at the other men. Now she has been claimed, their attentions have returned to their conversations. "Outside," she murmurs.

The man nods, making his way towards the front of the tavern. Scarlett grabs his arm.

"We can't go out the front door," she says, her fingers kneading his arm. "There's a man in there I turned down. Didn't like the look of him."

He grins. "And you like the look of me?"

"Very much." She gives him a syrupy smile. Ignores the skin prickling at the back of her neck.

He reaches brashly for her hand, sliding sausage fingers between hers. "The least we can do for the poor fellow is say goodbye."

She sidles closer to him, her skirts brushing over his boots. "Is that what you're here for? To bother yourself with other men?" She gives him doe eyes. "Or to bother yourself with me?"

One corner of his lips turns up as he considers her. "There's no other way out."

She smiles coyly. "Ayes there is." Her heart is drumming. "I know what goes on in this place. I'm sure you do too."

The man hesitates. After a moment, he gives a faint nod. Leads her towards the enormous stone hearth. No fire in the grate. No wood. No ash.

He steps over the grate and turns, disappearing from view. Scarlett bunches her skirts in her fist and follows him into the fireplace. To the side of the grate, a narrow hole has been beaten into the stone. Through it, she can hear the sigh of the sea.

She squeezes out of the hole, finding herself on a narrow path between the wall of the tavern and the cliff face. Clever, she thinks. The tavern is built in such a way it looks to be leaning against the rock. No one would ever know a path ran behind it.

In the splintered moonlight, the man is little more than an inky shape. He comes towards her, pressing her back against the rock. His stale breath is hot against her cheek. Seized with panic, Scarlett fumbles beneath her skirts for the knife. The man's fingers dive beneath her petticoat, squeezing the bare flesh above her stockings and making sickness rise in her throat. She yanks the blade from her garter and holds it to his throat. His hands fall.

"What is this?" he hisses.

Scarlett feels her breath come thick and fast. She has not thought this through. Unless she cuts the man's throat, he will come after her. He will go back to the tavern and spread word that the press gang's passage has been discovered. What choice does she have but to kill him?

The knife trembles in her fist. She does not want to be a killer. Does not want to leave a dead man in her wake, the way her father had done.

She does not want to be Jacob.

"What do you want?" the man spits. "Money?"

She hesitates. He cannot know she has any interest in the press gang. Before she can speak, he says:

"I've coins in my pocket. Let me get to them." His hand edges towards his pocket, her knife still hard against his throat.

Scarlett drives her knee into his groin and runs, leaving him hissing and cursing behind her. She tears through the narrow chasm between the rock and the tavern, then follows the path up a winding hill. Hidden by darkness at the top of the cliff is the blue and gold carriage she had seen the night Asher had escaped. There are no windows in the coach, she realises. How had she not noticed this the last time she had seen it?

She edges towards it. In the near darkness, she sees the box seat is empty. She moves silently towards the carriage and opens the door, willing herself not to make a sound. A crumpled figure lies on the floor. Asher. Her breath catches at the sight of him. He is sprawled on his side, taking short, shallow breaths. His hair is matted and tangled with straw. His eyes are closed, but he shows no sign of injury.

Scarlett kneels over him, rocking his shoulder. "Asher."

No response.

She presses her fingers to his neck. His pulse is fast. She leans close, trying to catch the scent of tainted brandy on his breath. The sweet waft of hay lining the floor of the carriage masks everything else.

Footsteps come towards the coach. Scarlett shifts, trying to bury herself in the shadows. The carriage creaks as men climb into the box seat.

"Go," someone calls to the driver.

"We can't. The judge wants two men."

"Can't find anyone else tonight," says the first voice. "Customs are in the tavern. One's the best we can do. Take him to the stables."

And the coach begins to move. Asher stirs and groans.

"Quiet," she hisses.

"Scarlett?" He doesn't open his eyes. "Help me."

The carriage stops. Scarlett presses an ear to the side of the coach, trying to catch hold of any sound that might give away their location. The sigh of the sea is gone. An owl coos. Footsteps. She wriggles beneath the bench.

The door creaks open and lamplight falls across Asher's face. Scarlett sees the legs of the men that climb into the carriage and grab his limp body. Hears him groan as he is hauled into the night.

The door slams and she lets herself breathe.

When the footsteps have faded, she slips out of the carriage. In the darkness, it is hard to make out her surroundings, but light glows beneath the doorway of a large, weather-beaten outbuilding. A cart shed? She hears mumbled voices. Men. They swing closed a heavy wooden door at the front of the building.

Where had they found Asher? Is he too to be thrown onto a naval ship and carted off to war? A fitting punishment for abandoning her, she thinks wryly. A fitting punishment for seeking to turn she and Isaac over to the revenue men.

There is a crack beneath the door of the cart shed. She presses herself to the muddy ground. She can see boots moving. How many men? Five perhaps? Six? Is the magistrate among them, paying the impressers for their services? Are there men from the navy here, come to collect their new recruit? The boots are ragged. None that look to belong to a magistrate, or naval officers.

Scarlett hears more footfalls. This time, they are sloshing through the mud outside the shed. Coming towards her. She scrambles to her feet and begins to run, her boots sliding in the mud. And a thick arm is around her waist, the man's other hand over her mouth to stop her scream escaping.

ABANDONMENT

Scarlett kicks wildly. She thrashes against her captor, trying to see his face. He flings her onto the ground outside the stables. Pain shoots up her side.

"Who in hell are you?" he hisses, his bearded face looming over her.

"I'm no one. I saw nothing. I—" She tries to stand, but the man pulls a pistol. Cocks the trigger. And in a sudden flash of movement, he falls, a fist slamming into the side of his head.

Jacob stands over the motionless body. "Run, Scarlett."

She stares at him, frozen.

His eyes flash. "Go!"

She scrambles to her feet and races towards the lights of the village. There are footsteps behind her. Heavy, growing closer. She keeps running. Hears him call her name. Lungs blazing, she stops running and lets him catch her.

"You knew who I was."

Jacob lowers his eyes. "Of course." He is breathless. "You're the image of your mother."

Her anger flares. A thousand questions well up inside her. She feels hot and cold at once. The Wild beats around inside her, making her head and heart pound.

Before she can order her thoughts, Jacob says: "You can't be anywhere near this place. It's not safe."

Scarlett doesn't move. "Why did you pretend not to know me?"

He snatches her arm and begins to walk further down the hill, leading her away from the press gang's hideout.

"Let go of me!" She thrashes against him.

He lets his hand fall, but keeps walking. "These men will kill you if they find you. Your seeing them has compromised their secrecy."

"I shouldn't be surprised to find you with your hands in such things," she spits. "Is this where free trade takes you now? To impressment? Taking blood money from a crooked magistrate?"

Jacob keeps walking. And stops. They are at his cottage with its overgrown front path. She has walked the entire way beside him, Scarlett realises.

"I'll answer all your questions," he says, unlocking the door. "I'll tell you whatever you want to know. But I'll not do it in the street. I can't risk those men finding you."

In spite of herself, Scarlett follows him inside. Jacob lights the lamp and sets it on the mantle. He has cleaned some of the mess she had made. The shattered jar of witch-powder has been swept up, the broken windows patched with rags. She feels a fleeting stab of guilt. Jacob gestures to a stool beside the table.

Scarlett sits hesitantly. Her father drags a storage trunk across the room and perches on the edge, facing her. His face is leathery beneath his beard; lines where there had not been lines, hollows in his once round cheeks. He is a strange phantom copy of the father she had known.

She feels his eyes on her, taking her in. Her skirts are caked in mud, her hair windswept and tangled. She is still without her shortjacket, she realises sickly, her breasts straining against her overtight stays. She yanks closed her cloak.

"What were you doing at the cart house?" he asks. "Was it me you were looking for? Or the man you call Asher Hales?"

She pins him with cold eyes. "I'm the one asking the questions."

Jacob looks down. "I'm a coward," he says. "That's why I pretended not to know you. You caught me by surprise. It was all I could think to do." His voice is thin. He does not sound the way she remembers.

She balls her hands into angry fists. "You're more than a coward."

He nods slowly. "How did you find me? Was it Asher Hales?"

Scarlett pushes past his question. "The press gang has him. Was that your doing?"

"He found work on a farm owned by one of the men in the gang. The man told me he'd hired a new worker. After you came to my cottage and told me Hales was in Portreath, I became suspicious."

"So it was your doing."

"He'll not be taken to the navy. Not yet at least. Not until he knows I'm the one responsible for his capture. I need him to know that."

Scarlett snorts. "Was it not enough for you to leave him on the beach with a murdered man?"

Jacob looks at his hands. "I want to explain to you about that night on the beach, Scarlett."

"You think I care one scrap about that night on the beach? You left us! We thought you dead!" Her voice rattles. "Your lies killed Mamm. She thought you had drowned and it broke her heart. And—"

"Your mother is dead?" Jacob interrupts.

Scarlett feels a sudden pain in her throat. For a long time, neither of them speak. Outside the cottage something rustles in the grass.

"I'm sorry, my girl," Jacob says finally. "More than you could know."

She shakes her head. "How can you say you're sorry when you're out here doing what you're doing? Pretending Isaac and I don't exist? Do you have any idea of the life you left for us?" She stands abruptly. "Leave me alone. I don't want a thing to do with you."

"Then why did you come to Portreath?"

Her heated reply falls short. "It was a mistake," she says finally, her voice catching. She swallows, determined not to cry in front of him.

Jacob stands and reaches for her arm again. This time, she lets him take it. His fingers are gentle against her bare wrist.

"What can I do?"

She stares at her feet. "You can come back to Talland and tell Charles Reuben you're alive. Tell him the debt belongs to you and not to Isaac."

Jacob looks down. "I can't go back to Talland. I'm sorry."

She pulls away. "Why not?"

"It's complicated."

"Why?"

"Because I'm a coward. I can't face Reuben. And I can't face your brother."

"That's not so complicated," Scarlett hisses, pulling open the door.

"You can't go back out there."

"No one has followed us."

"You don't know that. The men—"

"The men are dangerous, ayes. Are you not one of them? Are you not a part of the press gang? Why should I believe I'm any safer here with you?"

Jacob frowns. "Scarlett, please. I—"

"You've made it quite clear you want nothing to do with us," she snaps. "And you'll have your wish. I've spent most of my life believing you dead. I'll have no trouble convincing myself this is still the case."

She leaves the cottage without looking back. Perhaps there are men following her. Perhaps they have pistols in their hands, ready to put a bullet in her brain for finding their cart shed and their prisoner and their passage behind the inn. But she doesn't care.

She walks until she reaches Jamie's cottage.

"I know where the press gang is operating," she says when he opens the door.

He ushers her inside. "Did you go to the tavern again?" Scarlett hears a flicker of impatience in his voice.

She plants her hands on her hips. "Do you wish to know where the gang is operating or not?"

He nods. "Tell me."

And so she tells him of the drug-infused brandy, of the windowless carriage and the man in the powdered wig. Tells him of the passage through the fireplace and the cart shed on the hill where sailors are handed to the magistrate and sold on to the navy.

She says nothing of Asher Hales, or her father.

"How do you know all this?" Jamie asks.

She doesn't reply.

After a moment, he nods resignedly. "I'm glad you're safe."

Scarlett shivers. She crouches by the hearth and stares into the flames. And for the first time, she begins to see that the life she has built is a dangerous one. She thinks of the knife at her knee and the wolf eyes of Tom Leach and the lightless paths through the hills she has been running since she was a child.

Violence on the rise, Jamie had told her. Yes, she had heard of conflicts across the country. Had caught hold of stories passed between Isaac and his crew. The Hawkhurst Gang in the east. The riding officers strung up for murder last month while defending themselves in Looe. And yet somehow, she has managed to remain blind to the brutality of smuggling, even while rage at Leach and his men made her blood hot and her thoughts wild.

She hugs her knees.

"Was there a prisoner?" Jamie asks. "In the barn?"

She nods. A prisoner, yes. An anonymous, nameless prisoner.

"What will you do?" she asks. "Now you know where the press gang is operating? Do you have the authority to arrest them?"

Jamie begins to pace. "I have the authority to arrest them for smuggling."

"What do you mean? Those men weren't smuggling."

"No. But I can make it look as though they were. Seized contraband is brought into the customs station regularly. I can sneak out a haul and hide it at the cart shed." He looks at her with hot eyes. "When we know the gang is in there, I'll tell the other officers I've received a tip-off. They'll find the contraband and make the arrest."

Make the arrest. Arrest her murderer of a father.

Scarlett leans back against the leg of the table. "I always knew the revenue service was crooked."

Jamie chuckles, catching the short smile in the corner of her lips. "Those men deserve all that comes to them."

Guilt at her abandonment of Asher gnaws at the back of her mind. He would not be thrown onto a naval ship tonight, her father had told her. What worse fate did the press gang have in mind for him? Perhaps she ought to tell Jamie. Perhaps they ought to try and rescue him.

No. She had risked her life for him once and look where it has led her. To hell with him. He can find his own way out of the press gang's grasp.

She pushes away her guilt. Asher Hales is not worth guilt.

Jamie slides a stool to the fire and sits close to her. "How did you know?" he asks again. "I'll not be angry. I just want to know. I've been trying to catch those men out for months. I knew the impressed men were disappearing from the tavern, but it was the naval officers themselves taking them to the ships. I knew there had to be a place where the gang kept the men before handing them over. A place where they could liaise with the magistrate and collect their earnings."

"One of the men gave me a glass of brandy when I went to the inn that first night. There were something not right about it. A strange smell… I remembered what you said about the impressed men being drugged and…"

"But the hole in the fireplace," he pushes. "How did you find it?"

Scarlett avoids his eyes. "Someone showed it to me."

"Showed it to you?"

She hesitates, then looks at him with a wry smile. "It seems some men become quite trusting when they think a girl is going to lift her skirts." Her cheeks blaze.

Jamie starts to chuckle, making her laugh too.

"I thought you looked a little different," he says, trying far too hard to keep his eyes averted from her chest.

Scarlett takes her shortjacket from her pocket and slides it on hurriedly.

He touches her shoulder. "Stay here tonight."

"You have a watch?"

"No. But I can sleep on the floor."

"I couldn't."

"Why? Because it wouldn't be proper, or you don't want to risk another night in a riding officer's clutches?"

"Both."

He sighs slightly. "I thought we were past such distrust."

How she longs to be past it. How she longs to look into someone's eyes without trying to sift the truth from the lies.

"You know," Jamie tells her, poking at the fire, "I'm risking a lot by trusting you too."

"Why?"

"You've seen my journal. You could easily have read it when you were here alone last night. Could have sold my secrets to the Portreath traders."

"Then you're a fool to trust me."

"Perhaps." He presses a warm hand to her forearm. Scarlett feels something move in her chest. "Stay. You may not believe it, but I can assure you you're much safer here with me than out on the hills."

She hesitates. Her legs are aching with exhaustion, her mind craving the relief of sleep. Her bed in Redruth feels half the world away. "I'll take the floor," she says. "I insist."

Jamie pulls the blanket from the bed and hands it to her. "Then you'll take this at least."

"Do you have another?"

"I have my coat." He kicks off his boots and curls up on the sleeping pallet, pulling his broadcloth coat over his body. He rolls over and blows out the lamp. Scarlett lays the blanket by the hearth and cocoons herself in it. The fire is warm against her cheek. She turns, finds herself watching Jamie. The coat barely covers him; his knees pulled to his chest and his stockinged feet uncovered.

Scarlett stands. She slides the cloak from her shoulders and slips it over his body. He looks up. Smiles. Catches her eye in the glow of the flames.

She returns his smile faintly, then crawls back to her blanket beside the hearth. She lets her heart slow. Lets the crackle and sigh of the fire still her feverish thoughts. The flames die away and soon the only sound in the room is the in and out of breath. And how calming it is, Scarlett realises, to hear this riding officer's breathing rise and fall beside her own.

FLOWERS AND FIRE

The light is good here in Jack's room. In the day, the sun fills it, unlike the constant shadows that lie over so much of the inn. This is a better place for drying herbs. Flora goes to her mother's room and takes down the strings of plants. She ties them to the handle of the wardrobe in Jack's room and stretches them upwards towards the mantle. The sun has sunk now, and a fire is crackling in the grate. Below, the inn is quiet. Today is a day of rest.

These rooms had been guest chambers in the days when Flora's grandfather had run the Mariner's Arms. She had always planned to use them for the same purpose. But perhaps not. Perhaps in her inn they might have a different use.

Word has begun to spread that there are healing herbs drying in the village tavern. There have been people at the door, seeking cures for aches and coughs and pains. Men at the bar asking for tonics along with their liquor. Being of use, Flora is coming to realise, is a fine thing.

The floor creaks as Bessie appears in the doorway.

"Why are you out of bed, *cheel-vean*? It's late."

Bessie pokes at the flower fronds gently. In the golden light they are silhouettes, their spider leg shadows dancing over the walls. "I want to watch."

Flora makes her way along the line of hanging plants, touching the leaves, testing their dryness. What would Jack think if he could see her? She pushes the thought away. It doesn't matter. Jack is not here. Not in this room, not in this house, not in the tunnel. She hands the dried leaves to Bessie.

Careful now. Gentle. She hears her mother's words come from her mouth.

She brings the chest from the corner and opens the lid. Kneeling together in the red-yellow light, she and Bessie place them into pouches.

"What's this one? And this one?"

Flora tells her daughter the names of each. Mallow, angelica, yarrow.

Bessie lifts the black mirror from the chest. "What's this?"

Flora hesitates. "Your *mamm-wynn* used to say it was a magic mirror. She used it to try and see the future."

Bessie's blue eyes light. "See the future? Can you really do that, Mammik?"

Of course not, Flora would have said a month ago. *A mirror cannot tell the future.*

Instead: "I don't know."

Bessie peers into it.

"What do you see?"

"Just myself. And the flowers and the fire."

Flora smiles. She is glad Bessie has her father's rationality.

Jack feels suddenly close. What has triggered it? This faint regret over the scent of yarrow replacing his tobacco and brandy smell? Or is it the guilt she feels when she thinks of Isaac's hands running over her skin? Guilt at lifting the covers of their marriage bed and letting another man slide beneath.

"Bedtime," she tells Bessie, suddenly flustered.

With her daughter in bed, Flora is restless. There are accounts to do, but her mind is far too preoccupied. She walks through the still bar, her boots beating a rhythm on the flagstones. She has the mirror in her hand, she realises. Why has she brought it with her?

Her collection of seashells sits on the shelf above the cups. She takes down the shell Isaac had found for her in the cave, running her thumb over its pearly surface.

She cannot let herself fall for this man. No good can come of it.

Cannot fall for this man.

But she knows the futility of trying to talk herself out of it. She had fallen for Isaac Bailey when they were children building castles in the sand.

She and Jack had never spoken about what would happen if one of them were to die. That was a conversation for the old, the sick. They had been far too young and lovestruck to consider their own mortality.

Flora is sure Jack would want her to find happiness again. She is not yet thirty-two. With luck, she has far too many years ahead of her to spend walking alone through empty rooms.

So in another life, she is sure Jack would be happy to see her with Isaac. But in this life, Isaac has Caroline. He has children and debts and he must leave Talland.

And so: *what are you thinking?*, she can hear Jack say. *What are you thinking?*, as loud and clear as if he were looking over her shoulder at the shell in her hands.

She feels the pull of the tunnel. With the looking glass in hand, she walks down into the darkness, running a hand along the wall to keep her bearings.

What are you thinking?

What is drawing her down here? What does she truly expect to find? She does not believe the dead will walk.

But nor had she believed in healing incantations. Had not believed tomorrow could be seen in the mirror.

Why are you losing hold of who you once were?

But is she losing herself or finding herself? She can't be sure.

She looks into the mirror. Searching for what?

Everything feels hazy; her beliefs, her sense of self, where this world ends and another begins. She wants clarity, she realises. Wants answers. And she will look anywhere to find them.

The tunnel is dark, the mirror dark. Nothing to see but black rock walls. Light bounces suddenly off the surface of the glass, filling the tunnel with a sudden hot glow.

"Flora?" Isaac's voice snaps her back to reality. He looks down at the mirror.

"What are you doing?"

What *is* she doing?

He takes her hand and walks with her back towards the inn. When they are out of the cellar, he takes the mirror and sits it face down on a table. He pulls her towards him, his lips crashing against hers.

Flora digs her hands into his hair, returning his kiss. It's a joy, she realises, to be here in the present, in this solid, earthly world. A joy to feel a man's breath on her skin, to feel herself touched in ways she hasn't been for two years. It's a joy to feel her body ache and burn, reminding her that she is bright among the living.

Upstairs, silent, dark. The sigh of clothing against the floor. No dead men in the looking glass, no one walking the tunnel. The rest of the inn is still. She hears only his sharp intake of breath and her muffled murmurs against his shoulder as the pleasure of it mixes with pain.

Soon he will be gone. And she knows it is his leaving that has brought them here. His leaving is what has allowed this to happen. Because soon he will be gone and the secret of this will disappear, die.

She lies with her head to his chest, his heart drumming close to her ear. She can see nothing but the inky outlines of their bodies. The dark makes it easy to hide. To forget and ignore the world hunting and panting around them.

A knock at the door and reality clatters back sharply.

"Flora Kelly?" A man's voice. Unfamiliar. "Open the door."

She fumbles in the blackness, snatching her shift from the floor. The bed creaks as Isaac sits, lighting the lamp.

"Let me answer it," he says, pulling on his breeches.

Flora laces her bodice with jittery fingers. "Don't be mad. No one can know you're here."

She hurries downstairs, heart thumping. Opens the door to find the excisemen.

She is detached from her body when they go to the wall and pull down the liquor licence. She watches them break the glass, pore over the contents, pry at the seal.

She hears the words.

Under arrest.

Can't register their meaning.

Forgery.

She feels the officers' hands around the tops of her arms. Her head swims.

Isaac's voice at the bottom of the stairs. "Get your damn hands off her."

Flora tries to pull away. "No need to manhandle me like an animal."

"I'm coming with you," says Isaac, buttoning his coat.

"No. You need to stay with Bessie." She glances at the looking glass teetering on the edge of the table. "And lock the mirror away."

WARFARE

The excisemen lead Flora to the wagon waiting outside the inn. One of the officers pulls open the door. "Inside."

She bundles her skirts in her fist and climbs into the cart. She sits on the dirty boards and hugs her knees to her chest. The carriage rattles up the hill, the lights of the Mariner's Arms disappearing into the darkness.

Flora's stomach turns over.

She will breathe. She will stay calm. Fear will accomplish nothing.

The wagon stops abruptly, jolting her forward. She hears the footsteps of the excisemen come towards her. The door opens and she climbs out into the night. They have arrived at the Polperro customs house. The men lead her into a small room with a wooden table in the centre. They sit on one side, nodding to a stool opposite.

"Sit."

She does. Her mouth is dry. "May I have some water?"

He pours a cup from the jug on the desk. Flora gulps it down. The water is preserved with rum and leaves a bitter taste in her throat.

"Who printed the licence for you, Mrs Kelly?"

She raises her eyebrows. "That's what you want? To take down a dishonest printer?"

"I suggest you be a little more cooperative. As it stands, you're facing charges of forgery and selling liquor without a licence. If you're found guilty, you'll likely face imprisonment. Perhaps transportation."

The thought of it makes heat flood her body. But she meets the officer's eyes, forcing steadiness into her voice. "A Cornish jury will not convict their own."

"Are you certain of that? Certain enough to risk incarceration? Risk losing your daughter?"

She swallows heavily. Certain? No. But she will not let them see her unease. "You know I'm guilty," she says. "You know my licence is forged. Why are you questioning me? Why not just take me before the magistrate?"

The officers exchange glances and she feels something shift inside her.

The first officer leans towards her. "You know of the murders that occurred in Lansallos recently, I'm sure."

She nods.

"The local riding officers tell me you have so far been unhelpful in their investigation."

"You're in league with them, are you? I suppose I ought not be surprised."

His eyes harden at her sharp tone. "We know well there's a smuggling syndicate operating out of Talland. A thing the revenue service is most eager to prove." He pours his own cup of water and takes a casual sip. "Isaac Bailey was at your inn tonight."

"Is such a thing a crime?"

The officer's lips turn up. "That entirely depends on what he was doing there." His chair creaks. "But adultery laws are of little interest to us. They are a matter for your own conscience."

Flora keeps her gaze steady, despite the fire in her cheeks. "Let's not bother ourselves with each other's consciences."

The officer folds his arms. "Was Isaac Bailey involved in the murders?"

"I've no idea. Why are you asking me? Don't you have an innkeeper in Lansallos you might threaten?"

"We've come to you because you're the one with the counterfeit licence," the officer says sharply.

Flora swallows.

"It is important for not only the men of the preventative service but also the safety of the villagers that we put an end to this increase in gang violence. As the murders took place so close to Talland, we have every reason to believe Isaac Bailey and the other smugglers in his syndicate were involved."

"It seems you've made up your mind," says Flora.

"Yes. But we need a witness. Someone willing to stand up in court and condemn these men."

"A witness?" She laughs coldly. "You know I wasn't in Lansallos the night of the murders. I was in Talland running my inn."

The officer doesn't reply at once. "You'll tell the court you witnessed the shootings."

Flora sits back in her chair. "I suppose I shouldn't be surprised by your corruption."

"You are in no position to be self-righteous, Mrs Kelly. You have knowingly broken several laws."

Flora lowers her eyes. The man is right, of course. "Who told you about my licence?" she asks.

"What makes you think anyone told us?"

She smiles wryly. "You knew all along, I suppose."

"We suspected as much. You were offered the chance to help the revenue service. Had you done so, we would never have come looking."

Flora wraps her arms around herself. How foolish she has been, rushing into reopening with the forged licence, risking she and Bessie's safety. She had been desperate to keep the Mariner's Arms open, just as Jack would have wanted. But Jack, of course, would not have wanted this.

The officer leans towards her. "We want this warfare between smuggling gangs stopped. So much so we would be willing to overlook an innkeeper with a counterfeit liquor licence."

"Isaac Bailey is a friend," Flora says sharply. "If you think I will turn him in to free myself, you are mistaken."

"Take her to the lockup," one officer tells the other. "Let her think it over in there for the night."

And she is dragged from the customs house with vice-like hands at the top of her arms.

The lockup is a tiny stone hovel on the edge of the green. The stocks stand beside it, stained with blood and dinted by stones. The officer pulls a ring of keys from his pocket and unlocks the door. There is nothing inside but a narrow wooden bench. The floor is strewn with mud and filth.

Flora steps inside before the officer puts a hand to her. She swallows hard, the stench of human waste turning her stomach. She presses her palm hard against the wall, determined not to show her fear. She shivers violently, wishing for a shawl or cloak.

"I trust you understand the situation, Mrs Kelly," the officer tells her, moonlight shafting over his face as he pulls on the door. "Keep silent and you'll face the magistrate. Name names and you'll go free."

MEETING

The morning light burns through Asher's eyelids and makes his head pound. He blinks tentatively. His mouth is dry. He can smell hay and earth. Is he on the farm? His blurry eyes see men's boots.

He tries to sit. His whole body is an ache. He slumps wearily against the wall. This is not the farm. To one side of him sits a blue and gold carriage, its windows covered. He is in someone's cart shed.

This is not the farm, but the man coming towards him is the farmer. His eyes are darting and his fingers dance. He is wearing the same patched waistcoat he has been since Asher had met him.

"What do you want?" Asher spits.

The farmer chuckles. "Took him long enough to come out of it."

Asher tries to move, tries to see who the man is speaking to. A wall of pain slams him as he turns his head. He blinks hard. "What did you give me?"

"Just a little opium."

"Opium?"

Just a little opium would not have left him unconscious all night. He remembers the burn of the brandy they had forced down his throat. The liquor combined with the drug would have made for a lethal combination. He ought to be dead. Cold sweat prickles his skin and he lurches to one side, retching into the hay.

As he moves, he sees the other man. A man he recognises at once.

Jacob Bailey steps close. Leans over him. His breath is hot and stale against his cheek. Asher's stomach rolls.

Jacob hauls him to his feet, then shoves him down again. Asher lands hard on his side, pain shooting through him and dizziness seesawing the world.

This is not the meeting Asher had imagined when he had stood on the deck of the *Avalon* and watched Cornwall crawl towards him. Not the meeting he had imagined when he had cajoled and courted Scarlett to lead him to her father. In the meeting with Jacob Asher had imagined, he had been the one with the power. He would raise a pistol, give a victorious smile. *Tell me how to find the hidden wealth of Henry Avery.*

But there is no wealth and no pistol and no power. Just pain in his side and hay beneath his head. Opium in his blood and sickness in his throat.

Yes, Jacob had wronged him, but the things Asher had done in retaliation were far worse. A fist to his stomach and his breath leaves him. He gasps, coughs. Jacob strikes him again. Again. Blood runs hot and salty down his throat.

He will die, Asher thinks. Today is the day he will die. Terror seizes him. He has always been fascinated by death.

But it is not so intriguing, he realises, when the death coming towards him is his own.

The farmer pulls Jacob away. "Leave the man in one piece or the judge won't pay."

Asher rolls onto his knees. Coughs out a line of spittle and blood.

Jacob produces a pistol from his coat. He leans over Asher, breathing heavily. Dirt is streaked along one weathered cheek. The wildness in his eyes suggests he has no intention of leaving Asher in one piece. "You brought my daughter here. Why?"

Asher coughs, pain shooting through his side. "She found you then. A pleasant reunion, I'm sure."

Jacob shoves the nose of the pistol into Asher's neck.

He inhales sharply at the pain. "You'll kill me then? To protect Scarlett from me? Believe me, you have things the wrong way around."

"I'm not going to kill you," says Jacob. "You're worth more to me alive than dead. The navy pays well for a man with sea legs."

Asher feels fresh heat course through him. The world feels colourless and unsteady. He stands, stumbles. He feels the farmer's hands around the tops of his arms. He tries to struggle against them, but his muscles are weak with opium and fear. If he is not to die here, he will die with a touch rod in his hand, fighting for a country who had cast him from her shore.

Jacob stands close, pressing the gun to Asher's stomach. "It will be a great thing when a Spanish bullet takes you down. I don't want a thing more to do with you, or that hedge whore of yours."

Asher begins to laugh slowly, humourlesly. A Spanish bullet, he realises, is worth it, just to be the one to deliver the news. "That hedge whore has married your son."

BURIED TREASURE

The gun teeters in Jacob's hand. "You're lying," he says finally. "My son would not be so foolish as to go near that witch."

"Caroline," Asher says tautly. "Her name is Caroline. And no. I'm not lying. As much as I wish I were."

Jacob looks at the farmer. "Leave us. I'll take him to the judge when I'm done with him."

And the two men are alone. Jacob begins to pace. Asher eyes the doorway. Eyes the pistol. He will never make it. The opium is still playing with his legs.

"Why are you here with Scarlett?" Jacob asks after a long silence.

Asher wipes the blood trickling from his lip. "Because your dear daughter put a knife to me. Forced me to help her find you."

"You're a liar."

"I am a liar," says Asher. "But I'm telling the truth about this. Scarlett has your blood running through her. How can you be surprised she has a violent side?"

Jacob turns away.

"She's an anger in her like I've never seen," Asher continues, relishing the man's discomfort. "I'll warrant she gets that from you. Was it that wild anger that drove you to kill Albert Davey when he told you Avery's haul was a myth?"

Jacob doesn't look at him. "It's no myth."

"Of course it is."

"Believe what you like."

Asher shifts. Dare he try and believe again? A faint flicker of hope sparks inside him, quelled suddenly by the pistol hanging from Jacob's fist. Pain begins to pulse behind his eyes. "Why kill Davey?" he asks finally.

"Because I needed his money. What choice did I have but to kill him?" Jacob speaks plainly, without emotion.

What had he been thinking, Asher wonders, involving himself with such a man all those years ago? Little wonder his life has taken the course it has. But he is unable to push aside his curiosity. The pull of Avery's haul has taunted him for far too long for him to turn away now.

"Davey told you where the haul was hidden?"

Jacob nods faintly.

"Then why did you not claim it?"

"You know why." When he turns back to face Asher, Jacob's eyes are hard. "I've heard enough from you. It will be a great pleasure to sell you off to the navy after all you've cost me." He raises the pistol, nods towards the door. "Walk."

"We both want the same thing," Asher says hurriedly. "We both want Caroline away from Isaac."

His words are ones of desperation, but he is surprised to find he believes them. He would leave Talland, he had told Caroline, the morning he had returned from Isaac's trading run to Guernsey. He would leave her to her miserable life of patched skirts and broken windows. Would leave her to watch as her husband was strung up for smuggling. She would become nothing more to him than a memory.

But he sees now, somewhere not-so-deep inside, he had had no intention of leaving her. Caroline is as important to his perfect life as Avery's money.

He had tried to convince himself he could have the life of his dreams without her in it. Fill the hole she had left with a dazzling career and a string of beautiful women. But now she is back in his life, he sees he can do no such thing. As hard as he has tried to ignore it, he knows the passion he'd felt for her when they were teenagers is still raging inside him.

He watches Jacob pace across the cart shed. "We've wanted the same thing in the past," he tells Asher tautly. "But it seems we are unable to cooperate."

Unable to cooperate indeed. But Asher hears the roar of cannon fire, feels a touch rod in his hand. Smoke in his eyes, a watery grave.

"We can cooperate," he says, his voice thin with desperation. "We will go back to Talland and I'll bring Caroline to you. She'll not risk Isaac finding out what she did. She'll have no choice but to leave."

Jacob gives a snort of humourless laughter. "With you?"

Asher swallows. In the nearby stables, a horse sighs noisily.

"If I see her, I will kill her. Not hand her over to you so she can run away and live happily."

The knot in Asher's stomach tightens. Is this fear for Caroline? Or for himself? Jacob will have a bullet for each of them, he has no doubt. But his only hope of escaping the navy is to convince him they must return to Talland together.

"Kill her?" he says, forcing steadiness into his voice. "And do you expect Isaac will allow you back into his life if you burst into the village and murder his wife?"

Jacob doesn't look at him. "I'm quite sure I have no place in Isaac's life."

Asher sees Caroline with Jacob's bullet in her chest. Sees blood snake and pool across her body. Sees her eyes become glassy. He coughs down a fresh wave of sickness.

He cannot let himself be impressed. Cannot let Jacob take him to the magistrate. He will die and so will she. Convincing Jacob to ally with him is all the hope he has.

"You are so certain Isaac will turn you away?" says Asher. "Even if he knows the true reason you left?" He knows he is playing a dangerous game. Isaac Bailey is a hard man to read. There is no way of knowing how he would react if he were to find out the truth of why his father left. Does Isaac have it in him to kill those who have wronged him? Perhaps he would be safer fighting the Spanish, Asher thinks sickly.

Jacob paces across the shed. "I don't need you to get Caroline out of Isaac's life. Scarlett is in Portreath. I'll tell her everything. When she returns to Talland with that knowledge, Caroline will have no choice but to leave."

And another wave of fear comes. Scarlett knowing the true reason her father abandoned his family, Asher realises, is far worse than Isaac knowing. Scarlett is gunpowder hovering inches from a flame.

He forces out a chuckle. "And you think she will just believe you?"

"Why shouldn't she?"

"Because she despises you," Asher hisses. "She would happily see you dead and she'll not believe a word that comes from you."

"And if it came from you?"

"Then there is even less chance of her believing it."

Jacob folds his hands behind his head. "Where can I find her?"

"I've no idea."

"Don't lie to me! You're the one who brought her here."

"And I've been lying unconscious in this cursed shed since yesterday. I've no idea what's become of Scarlett."

For a long time, Jacob doesn't speak. Asher's heart thuds. "You need me," he says desperately. "You want rid of Caroline, I need to be involved. You know I'm right."

Jacob grabs Asher's arm and shoves him forward. Pins the pistol into his spine. "Walk."

And Asher walks on unsteady legs out of the cart shed and down a winding hill. The sea stretches out beneath him, beating ceaselessly at stacks of black rock.

They walk until they reach a tiny shack a few yards back from the road. Jacob unlocks the door and shoves Asher inside. He forces him onto a stool and uses a length of rope to bind his wrists and ankles.

Jacob makes for the door without speaking.

Is he going to seek out his daughter? Tell her his real reasons for leaving Talland? If Scarlett believes his story,

Asher is of no value. He will be thrown onto a naval vessel and Jacob Bailey will have his revenge.

He prays Scarlett's untrusting side is still intact.

WITNESSES

"Two minutes." The excise officer opens the door of the lockup, letting Isaac inside. Flora leaps to her feet, squinting in the sudden, muted sunlight. The door slams and the dark returns abruptly.

"Bessie. Is she—"

"She's safe. She's with us." Isaac pulls her into his arms. "You're frozen," he says, feeling her shiver against him. He slides off his coat and pulls it over her shoulders. "Did they hurt you?"

She shakes her head. Pulls the coat tighter around her. "They want me to name names. Tell them I witnessed the murders." Her breath plumes in a silver cloud. "They suspect you, Isaac. But they've no proof. No witnesses." She rubs her eyes. "I'm surprised they let you see me."

"And if you turn me over to them? They'll free you?"

She gives him a withering look. "You know I'd never think of it."

Isaac begins to pace, his thoughts charging. He'd not managed an hour of sleep. His boots slide through the muck on the floor of the lockup. "Tell them you saw Leach kill the riding officers."

Flora looks at her feet. "I couldn't."

"Leach killed those men," Isaac hisses. "I saw him do it."

"Yes, but I did not."

He lets out his breath in frustration. He lifts Flora's arm, where the cut from Leach's knife is still strapped tightly. "Have you forgotten what he did to you? You owe the bastard no loyalty!"

"I'll not lower myself to his level."

"Not even to save yourself?"

She turns away, her jaw clenched and her eyes hard. Isaac burns with a thorny mix of frustration and respect. "You've lied to the revenue men before," he reminds her.

"A few petty lies are one thing. Turning a man in for murder is quite another." She wraps her arms around herself. "They can take me to trial. I'll not be found guilty by a magistrate who has drunk at my inn. The Cornish protect their own."

"You cannot possibly know that! The revenue men may well have had a word in the magistrate's ear."

"Perhaps. But I'll not stand up in court and claim to have witnessed something I didn't see." Her voice is thick with exhaustion. "You may have given up on morality, Isaac, but I haven't."

He exhales in frustration. "Ayes, Flora, you're a damn picture of morality, with your forged licence and your smuggled liquor and…"

"The married man in my bed?"

165

Isaac sighs. He drops onto the bench and tugs her down beside him. He laces his fingers through hers and holds her hand against his chest to warm it. "You can't count on a lenient magistrate. The authorities want someone to pin the murders on. They want to make a point to other trading gangs. Give them what they want. Please."

She stares into the darkness, not speaking. He wonders what she is thinking.

The door creaks. "Time," the officer says curtly.

Isaac turns back to Flora and drops his voice. "Think of Bessie. Where would she be without you?" He squeezes her hand. "Where would *I* be without you?"

She lets out her breath, pulling her fingers from his. "Where would you be? You will be far from Talland with your wife and children, Isaac. That is where you will be." She slips his tarred fishing coat from her shoulders. "Take it."

"Don't be foolish. You're shivering."

"And what will you wear?" She drops her voice. "That greatcoat covered in John Baker's blood?"

The officer gestures for Isaac to leave. He takes the coat reluctantly and stands outside the lockup, simmering with frustration.

Reuben's mansion blots the hill. Just the sight of it makes Isaac angry. But Reuben will be another voice trying to talk Flora towards reason.

He climbs up to the house and knocks on the door. "I need to speak with Reuben urgently," he tells the maid. She ushers him inside and disappears down the hall.

After a moment, Reuben appears from the parlour. He is in his shirtsleeves, his head bald without its customary white wig.

"Mr Bailey," he says stiffly. "I'm surprised to see you here." His voice is curt and clipped.

"Flora needs your help."

The hardness in Reuben's eyes vanishes. "What's happened?"

Isaac tells him of the excisemen's visit, tells him of the arrest.

Reuben exhales. "I should never have helped her obtain that licence."

Isaac says nothing. As much as he longs to blame Reuben, he knows Flora would have gotten her hands on a licence with or without his help. "They've offered her freedom if she names the traders involved in the murders." He must tread carefully. Reuben cannot know of his involvement. "They've asked her to lie to the magistrate in order to put an end to the warfare between traders."

"I take it she will not agree."

"She's stubborn. Trying to cling to a little morality."

Reuben gives a short chuckle. "Aren't we all." He rubs his chin. "You believe Tom Leach and his men were involved?"

Isaac nods. "Flora knows this. But she'll not turn him in. She'll not condemn a man on hearsay."

Reuben lets out his breath. "Her decency is misplaced as far as Leach is concerned."

"She's counting on a lenient magistrate in Polperro," Isaac tells him. "She's telling herself she'll not be convicted by a man who has drunk at her inn."

Reuben reaches for a greatcoat hanging on a hook beside the door. "Then she needs to believe she will face a magistrate from outside these parts."

Flora is surprised to see Reuben enter the lockup. "How did you know I was here?"

"Your friend Mr Bailey told me."

She shivers. "Did he have you come here and convince me to turn Tom Leach in?"

"I've come on my own accord, Mrs Kelly. I do not act on Isaac Bailey's bidding." Reuben stands in the doorway, eying the filth-covered floor. He reaches into his pocket and hands her an apple. "Here. I thought you may be hungry."

"Thank you." Flora's stomach is rolling. She is not sure if it is hunger or fear.

Reuben stays with his back pressed to the door. "As you may know, I am well acquainted with this town's magistrate. When I heard of your arrest, I sought him out. The revenue service are always quick to take a prisoner to trial. I wanted to know when you will be facing the court."

She stiffens. "And?"

"And he knows nothing of your case. From this I could only assume he would not be the one overseeing the trial. I spoke to the men who arrested you at the inn last night. And I'm afraid my suspicions are correct. They plan to take you to trial in Exeter."

She feels suddenly hot and dizzy. "What?" she manages.

"Your trial is important to them," says Reuben. "They don't want a biased magistrate."

She begins to pace. "They don't care about my trial. They just want to pressure me into lying about witnessing the murders."

"Yes. That's exactly why your trial is important to them."

A line of sweat runs down her back. "When?"

"They plan to take you to Exeter tomorrow morning."

Flora sits, her legs weakening. She stares at the strip of light pushing beneath the door. The constant darkness is tangling her thoughts.

"I'm sure I need not tell you, you cannot rely on leniency from a magistrate outside of Cornwall," says Reuben. "And I'm sure the revenue men have made you aware of the penalties for forgery."

She nods faintly. Imprisonment. Transportation. She will be torn from her life, her home, her inn strung with flowers.

She will be torn from her daughter.

What will happen to Bessie? The children's home? Is she to grow up among orphans because her mother pretended she had morals?

She can't let such a thing happen.

She will do this for her daughter, she tells herself. Will do it for Bessie. Yes, she can find a justification for immorality. A validation for lies in the witness stand. There is always a justification if you look hard enough.

"Tell the officers I wish to see them," she says, avoiding Reuben's eyes. Her voice comes out sounding like someone else.

"I'll do that," he says. She catches a faint smile in the corner of his lips.

She is pacing the lockup when they arrive.

"Yes, Mrs Kelly? Is there something you wish to tell us?"

She draws in her breath and lifts her chin. Forces a steadiness into her voice. "I saw Tom Leach kill the riding officers in Lansallos."

RETRIBUTION

The windowless carriage sits at the top of the hill. Light flickers in the tavern below.

Scarlett waits at the edge of the quay for Jamie. He needs to hurry if they are to plant the contraband in the cart shed tonight. The moment the press gang seize their target, the carriage will be on the move and their chance will be lost.

She turns abruptly at the sound of footsteps. Jamie is in uniform, ready for his watch later that night. His hands are dug into the pockets of his coat, wind blowing dark waves of hair back from his face. Scarlett is not sure if she is comforted or unnerved by a man striding towards her with brass buckles on his boots. He grins at the sight of her and she finds herself returning his smile.

She looks back at the tavern as muffled laughter sounds through the windows. "The innkeeper must know what's going on this place."

Jamie turns up the collar of his coat. "No doubt he gets a cut in exchange for his silence." He pulls a package from his pocket and hands it to Scarlett. "Put it in your cloak." There is a crooked smile in the corner of his lips.

"What is it?"

He grins. "Tobacco." He gestures to his own overflowing pockets. "I've jewels and lace. Anything bigger was too difficult to get out of the customs store without being seen." He nudges her shoulder. "I thought you'd like the tobacco. Old time's sake and all."

Scarlett hesitates.

Jamie's smile disappears. "Truly? You doubt me?"

She swallows hard. No. If she is to walk into a trap, she will do it in pursuit of her old, trusting self. She slides the tobacco into her pocket. "Of course not." Her voice is trapped in her throat.

Jamie touches her elbow. "Show me how to find the cart shed."

The house in front of the shed is dark. A lamp swings in the breeze above the front door, but the windows are lightless. Scarlett slips through the gate and leads Jamie towards the cart shed. He heaves open the thick wooden door and slips inside. Shoves the bundles of lace and jewels behind a shelf stacked with oil tins.

"What will you tell your colleagues?" Scarlett asks, handing him the tobacco. "Will you admit you set the men up?"

"Never. I'd be strung up myself. I'll just tell them I have my suspicions about the place. Request assistance with a raid."

"And if they discover the contraband came from Customs House?"

"Then the press gang will be charged with theft of government property." He turns to face her. "I'm sure you don't think well of me. You've seen more than one of my underhand tactics." She hears a flicker of light in his voice.

"You're doing this for your brother," says Scarlett. "I understand." After a moment, she says: "I'd do the same." She feels a sudden, desperate urge to see Isaac. She longs to tell him all she has uncovered. Longs to tell him of the press gang and the cottage on the hill and the almost-regret in Jacob's voice. She cannot carry the weight of it alone.

She and Isaac had parted on terrible terms, but he will worry for her, of course. He always has. She can't shake her concern over him either. When last she had seen him, he had been sinking ships and speaking of escape. She hopes he is keeping his new recklessness out of Reuben's sight.

She follows Jamie from the shed. He goes to the front of the property and sits with his back against the stone fence surrounding the house. "You don't need to be here," he tells her.

She sits beside him. "I want to be." She needs to be a part of this, she realises. Needs to see Jacob punished. To Jamie, she says: "You could use the company."

He smiles. "This must feel like a betrayal to you. Working with the revenue men." There is playfulness in his voice and Scarlett knows he does not mean her to feel shame. She feels it anyway.

"It's the right thing to do," she says, hugging her knees.

Jamie raises a dark eyebrow. "I'm sure there are many who would disagree with you. I'll lose my job if anyone finds out what I've done."

"The right path is not always so clear," says Scarlett.

Jamie murmurs something soft, unintelligible. Hair blows across his eyes. Their breath is silver in front of them, disappearing into the thick of the night. And Scarlett begins to remember the power the darkness has over her; its ability to banish the Wild and bring a little peace. She feels the churning inside her begin to still.

What a strange thing, she thinks, that she might feel such calm as she sits beside a riding officer waiting to string up her father.

The right path is not always so clear.

Jamie shifts beside her, his shoulder knocking against hers. The contact sends an unexpected rush of energy down her arm. She pushes it away. Tomorrow the coach will leave for Talland and Jamie McCulley will become a memory.

"Right thing to do or not," he says, "I know you risked a lot to help me." He presses his gloved hand to her wrist. "I'm grateful." His fingers move against her arm and the fluttering inside her intensifies. She wants to slide closer. Wants to feel his hand move past her wrist. Under her cloak. Wants to feel those gloved fingers on her neck, her cheek, her lips. She realises she is holding her breath.

She feels him trying to catch her eye.

She has made mistakes around men before. Most notably, in the form of Asher Hales. She has let herself fall hard, fast and foolish. Mistakes.

Jamie would certainly be a mistake. But his hand is warm and restless, and the carriage will leave tomorrow. In the morning he will be a memory.

She turns to face him. His nose is close to hers. And his hand is sliding up her arm, beneath her cloak, slow and gentle and curious. Scarlett hears her breath catch.

The noise comes first. A rhythmic rattle as the windowless carriage pelts up the road.

Jamie pulls his hand away and leaps to his feet. "I'm going for the other officers. I'll take you back to my cottage on the way."

"No. You need to get the others as quickly as you can. I can make my own way back."

He hesitates. "All right. But promise me you'll go straight to the cottage."

Scarlett squints as the carriage draws closer. She can see her father in the box seat. She nods. Watches Jamie run into the dark.

Light spills from the front of the carriage and sways over the road. Scarlett hides behind the stone fence, keeping her head down as the coach rolls through the gates towards the cart shed.

She dares to look up. She will leave, yes. She has promised Jamie. But she can't take her eyes from her father. He climbs from the box seat and opens the carriage door. He tilts his head to stretch his neck, the way Scarlett remembers him doing when she was a child. Three men jump from the coach and haul out a limp body. Carry it towards the stables. And Scarlett walks deliberately towards the carriage. She wants Jacob to see her. Wants him to know, when the riding officers appear and haul him away, that she has had her retribution.

He catches sight of her as he is latching closed the carriage door. "You always were a brave thing," he says. "If more than a little foolish." She expects an eruption, but he gives a small smile and says: "I'm glad I found you." He puts a firm hand to the back of her neck and walks her towards the gate. "You need to leave. Asher Hales is not here. There are only men who would happily kill you."

Scarlett swallows heavily. Yes, she needs to pretend she is here to save Asher, or Jamie's plans will be ruined.

"Where is he?" she asks Jacob. "What have you done with him?"

"Don't waste your time worrying over that man. He's not worth it." He walks her towards the front gate. No, Jacob cannot leave. The riding officers will be here soon. She can't let him walk free.

"I need to speak with you," she says.

His fingers soften against the back of her neck. "Not here, Scarlett. It's too dangerous. I've told you before."

"Here," she says sharply. "Or nowhere."

Jacob sighs. Nods. He stands by the gate, one side of his face lit by the lamp above the front door. He looks at her expectantly. And so Scarlett asks him that which has been bubbling inside her since she first read Asher's letter.

"Did you ever truly love us?"

She hears a sound come from Jacob's throat. He stares out at the dark expanse of moorland beyond the house. His eyes are glassy. "I know you have no reason to believe me. But things are not as straightforward as you think. Everything I did was for you."

"You're right," Scarlett says coldly. "I don't believe you."

He sighs. "Isaac's wife. Tell me about her."

"Why?" When her father doesn't reply, Scarlett says: "She loves him. She loves him enough to have married into the debt you saddled us with. She loves him enough to settle for a life of poverty."

"And how does she treat you?"

Scarlett shrugs. "We will never be close. But she has always done right by me." She looks at him pointedly. "She was the closest I had to a mother. Perhaps I have not always been so grateful." She frowns. "Why do you care about Caroline?"

"I just want to know of your lives." Jacob looks distant. "Are there children?"

She lets out her breath. "If you want to know of our lives, you know how to find us."

"Tell me Scarlett! Are there children?"

"Yes," she says tautly. "Two."

For a long time, Jacob doesn't speak. Scarlett glances sideways at him. What is he thinking?

"And you," he says after a moment. "Are you surviving?"

She laughs coldly. "Surviving? Ayes. I get by with what little scraps Reuben decides to toss my way."

"That's not what I meant." Jacob turns to look at her. His eyes glow in the hot light. "I've a great anger inside me, Scarlett. An anger that makes me lose control. An anger that scares me." He swallows. "I know it's in you too."

She looks at her hands, unnerved by the intensity of his gaze. "You don't know a thing about me." She can feel Jacob's eyes on her. Refuses to look at him.

"When I became a father," he says, "I grew terrified of passing this anger on. I didn't want my sons and daughters to suffer as I had. I never saw it in any of my other children. But then you came along. And I watched that anger rear up inside you. I saw the darkness I feel within me show itself in your eyes."

Scarlett shifts uncomfortably.

"I let it take me over," Jacob says, "and I killed a man. I killed him because I wanted to steal from him. I was lucky I didn't hang for it. I don't want the same thing to happen to you."

Scarlett doesn't speak. She wants to, she realises. Wants to speak to the only person in the world who will understand. She wants to ask him if he too feels detached from his body when the Wild takes hold. Wants to know if the dark brings him peace. Wants to know if he has ever felt the anger take prominence, the way it has done for her these past few days. But she doesn't want to allow him in. Doesn't want him inside her head. He doesn't deserve it.

She feels him work his fingers through her hair, the way he had done when she was a child. The way he had done to calm her when the Wild seized her.

Tears well behind her eyes. The father she had thought she had lost is standing before her with his hands in her hair. How is it that she feels only bitterness? She pushes away a tear as it escapes down her cheek. "You left us with a debt we can never hope to repay," she says finally. "And it's your anger you're sorry for passing on to me?"

Hooves thunder suddenly up the path, along with a spear of light. Three horses charge through the gates, Jamie on one of them. He stops abruptly at the sight of Jacob and Scarlett, leaving the other officers to make for the cart shed.

He climbs from the horse and looks at Scarlett. "Why are you still here?"

Jacob eyes Jamie's uniform, then looks back at his daughter. "I can't be surprised at this, I suppose," he says, his voice strangely empty of emotion. "After all I've done to you."

Scarlett says nothing.

"You'll truly see your own father strung up?"

Her throat is tight. There would be a feeling of satisfaction when the riding officers came, she had been sure. But there is none of that. Just guilt. How dare he make her feel guilty after everything else he has done? She meets his eyes boldly.

"Go," Jamie tells Jacob.

Scarlett whirls around to face him. "What?"

"Quickly. Before the other officers find you."

Scarlett feels her father's eyes on her. She turns her back. And she hears his footsteps disappear out of the gate and thud down the hill. Hears her father run back into memory. She forces away the pain in her throat.

"Is that why you came to Portreath?" Jamie asks after a moment. "To find your father?"

Scarlett's tears spill and she swipes at them angrily. "Why did you let him go? He may have been the one who took your brother."

"You would have come to regret it if he was arrested because of you."

Damn Jamie and his decency. Damn him for shining a light on her failings.

"Don't pretend to know me," she hisses. "Or anything about my father." She feels hot and unsteady as she forces the rage to stay inside. Jamie cannot see the Wild. Not now. Not ever. From the cart shed, she hears the shouts of the revenue men. "Go inside," she tells him sharply. "Go and do your job."

She feels calmer by the time she makes it back to the village. She climbs up Battery Hill, stopping outside Mrs Acton's house. She reaches into her stays and pulls out the coins. What freedom this money would bring her. How much of the world she could see. But there is already far too much of Jacob in her. She does not want his greed too.

She sets the coins on the front step, still wrapped in the embroidered handkerchief. Mrs Acton will know who had taken them, she is sure. But at least she might begin to make amends.

She walks back down the hill. A thin line of dawn is pushing away the dark.

She has nothing now. Her only way back to Talland is to walk. But she would rather have nothing than carry pieces of her father inside her.

TRAVELLERS

Jacob throws open the door of his cottage. He is a violent stench of sweat and animals.

"You were right," he says, his fingers working at the knots binding Asher to the stool. "My daughter will not believe a word that comes from me." He pulls him to his feet. Slides the gun from his pocket. He is flustered. Angry. A mess.

"I cannot just walk up to my son's house and knock on the door. He'll cast me out before I manage a word." He jabs his pistol into Asher's spine and shoves him towards the door. "You will come back to Talland will me. Tell Caroline I wish to see her."

Scarlett's legs are already aching when she returns to Jamie's lodgings. Her eyes are heavy with sleeplessness. She has not yet even walked the hill out of the village. How distant Talland feels.

He opens the door before she knocks. He is still in his uniform shirt and breeches. "Where have you been? I was worried for you. I thought you were angry with me for letting your father go."

She doesn't look at him. "May I please have a little bread?"

He ushers her inside. Takes a loaf from the shelf and wraps it in a cloth. "You told me your father was dead," he says gently. "Why?"

Scarlett stares at her feet. "Because I wanted him to be." She blinks away her tears. "I know it a dreadful thing to say."

Jamie presses the loaf into her hand. "Stay a while. Rest. The coach doesn't leave for a few hours."

"I'm not taking the coach. I…" She draws in her breath. "I don't have my money anymore." She catches his eye for a moment and he nods silently. She is grateful he does not ask questions. She holds the wrapped loaf to her chest. "Thank you. For everything." She turns towards the door before he can respond. She knows if he tries hard enough he could convince her stay. She can't let such a thing happen.

She swallows a little of the bread, then sets out towards the hills. In the morning sun they shine and shimmer. The grass ripples as the wind skims through it. She must keep her wits about her as she walks.

She hears the rhythmic clop of hooves.

"Scarlett," says Jamie, "you can't walk all the way to Talland."

She looks up at him. He is wearing his broadcloth coat and long black riding boots, a scarf knotted at his neck. A bag is strapped to the saddle.

"You own a horse?" she asks throatily.

He smiles. "Yes. I'm a riding officer."

She begins to walk again. "Go home, please."

"Get on the horse."

Scarlett shakes her head. She can think of few worse ideas than taking a revenue man home with her.

"When we get to Talland, I'll turn around and come straight back, I swear it. I just want to see you there safely."

She squeezes her eyes closed. How desperately she wants someone to travel with. Someone to help her negotiate the maze of paths and hills and spirit-riddled streams.

But it cannot be this man.

She shakes her head.

"Why not?"

"Because of what I am. Because of what my family is. Turn us in and you would eat well for a year." As she speaks, she hears her own bitterness, her own doubt. She wants nothing more than to trust him. But the Wild refuses to release her. She puts her head down and quickens her pace. Jamie walks the horse beside her.

"My job is to patrol the coast between Portreath and Saint Ives. What happens in Talland is outside my jurisdiction."

Scarlett thinks of the false bottom in Isaac's lugger. Thinks of the tunnel snaking through the hill beneath the Mariner's Arms. "And I am to trust you not to hand over our secrets to your colleagues on the south coast?"

"Yes," Jamie says firmly. "You are to trust me."

Scarlett lets out her breath. "I want to," she says. "Truly. I want to trust you so badly."

"Well," he says, "the thing is, you can't stop me from riding all the way to Talland beside you. But if I'm to keep on at a walking pace, it will take far longer. So you may as well get on the horse."

Scarlett grits her teeth. Then, finally, she nods, letting Jamie pull her into the saddle. Feels the restlessness inside her begin to still at the warmth of his body pressed against hers.

EVIL SPIRITS

"I'm glad to see you," Reuben tells Flora. "Glad to see you free. You made the right decision."

Flora shifts edgily. Being inside Reuben's mansion makes her uncomfortable at the best of times. "My conscience thinks otherwise."

Reuben takes the pipe from his mouth and gestures to an armchair. "Tom Leach is not worth a guilty conscience, my dear."

Flora remains standing in the middle of Reuben's garish gold-rimmed parlour. She does not remove her cloak or woollen bonnet. "Some time ago you said you would buy my liquor back from me. Does that offer still stand?"

Reuben pulls himself from the chair. "You wish to sell your liquor?"

"What choice do I have? The excisemen know my licence was forged. I've no option but to operate as an alehouse."

He takes a step towards her. "Are you sure you'll not sit? Have a little tea? You're on edge. I can tell."

Flora grits her teeth. She has not slept. After the excisemen had released her, she had gone home and scrubbed herself clean. Set off to Reuben's the moment she was dressed. She wants nothing more than to make the necessary arrangements and be done with it. But being rude to Reuben will not help her cause.

She sits reluctantly. Reuben gives a self-satisfied smile and calls for the tea. He sits his pipe in an ash tray.

"The liquor," Flora says stiffly, "will you buy it back or not?"

"Of course. You know I'm a man of my word."

She gives a nod of thanks. "Will you have your men collect it? Five ankers are still unopened."

"The men will be there tonight. Perhaps I might join them. See how the tunnel is progressing."

Flora thinks of Isaac's brandy hidden in a bend of the passage. "There's been little progress," she says hurriedly. "There's nothing to see."

Reuben rubs his chin. "I'm sorry," he says after a moment. "I know the Mariner's Arms is very dear to you. I know you feel running the place as an alehouse will put you at a disadvantage against the inns in Polperro. But I'm sure you'll manage to keep it afloat. You've a passion for the place. And you're putting every penny towards purchasing a legitimate licence, I'm sure."

Reuben's condescension makes her want to shove his pipe in his eye. "Yes, well. Pennies can be few and far between."

He opens his mouth to speak, then pauses, his colourless lips parted. He laces his thick fingers across his middle. When he speaks, his voice has lost a little of its pretentiousness. "I could make a good life for you and your daughter, Mrs Kelly."

Flora's eyebrows shoot upwards. "I'm perfectly capable of providing for my daughter." Her voice comes out sharper than she had intended.

"Thanks to my generosity."

"You wish repayment for your assistance?"

"No," he says hurriedly. "Forgive me. I—"

Flora stands. Eyes the door.

"I didn't help you expecting anything in return," Reuben says hurriedly. "I merely..." He climbs from his chair to look her in the eye. "You and I, we've both lost a great deal." He swallows, shifting his weight between his brass-buckled feet. "I care for you, Flora. Very much. I would like the chance to show you."

The maid brings the tea tray into the room and sets it on the table. It clatters loudly in the silence.

"I'm sorry," Flora says, "Bess and I are happy as we are." A faint stab of remorse twists inside her. She has never seen this fragility in Reuben's eyes before.

He waits for the maid to leave, then steps closer, cupping her elbow. "A woman ought to have a man in her life. For security." She shifts uncomfortably and he removes his hand. "What would you do should the villagers turn on you again as they did recently?"

"I shall manage without you, as I did last time. I'm sorry Mr Reuben, I owe you no explanation."

"Very well." His cheeks are flushed. "You can expect my men this evening to collect the remaining ankers. I'll have payment for you once they are received."

Flora nods faintly. "Thank you."

He clears his throat. "The tea. Will you stay for a cup?"

"I don't think so." She hurries towards the door.

"Isaac Bailey is a married man, Mrs Kelly," Reuben says suddenly.

She feels a blaze in her cheeks. "This has nothing to do with Isaac," she snaps, keeping her back to him. She stops walking. Turns slowly. "The excisemen asked me why I had changed my mind," she says. "Why I decided to save myself by turning Leach in." She had planned not to raise the issue. But Reuben's mention of Isaac has stirred up her anger. "They seemed rather vague when I told them I did not want to be taken to trial in Exeter. They seemed to have little idea what I was speaking of."

Reuben fills a tea cup and brings it slowly to his lips.

"You lied to me," says Flora.

"That is quite an accusation."

She stares him down. "Are you saying I'm mistaken?"

Reuben smiles, but the warmth has disappeared from his eyes. The cup clinks loudly as he sets it back on the saucer. "I'm saying it is unwise to accuse those who clearly have your best interests at heart."

Her encounter with Reuben does not help Flora's sleeplessness. Her body is exhausted after a night shivering in the lockup, but her mind refuses to still.

The kitchen is filled with the sickly scents of apples and nutmeg. A pot of spiced ale bubbles on the range. Flora stirs it, tastes. It is far too sweet and lacking intensity.

Underwhelming.

An hour earlier, Reuben's men had taken the ankers of brandy from her cellar. If the Mariner's Arms is to survive as an alehouse, she'd best make lambswool a damn sight better than this. She tosses in a random handful of ginger.

There is a knock at the door. She stiffens. Visitors make her wary these days. She sets the pot on the table and makes her way downstairs. Peering through the keyhole, she sees the riding officers who had questioned her in Polperro the day after the shootings.

They will be bringing news of Tom Leach, she is sure. That afternoon, the officers had ridden to Polruan to bring in Leach for the murders. In two days' time, she will stand before the magistrate and lie. Send Leach to the scaffold to save herself.

Bessie, she thinks, *she is doing it for Bessie.*

But she knows the truth of it is far more complex. She is doing it for Bessie, yes, but she is also doing it to spare herself the prison cell she deserves.

The riding officers do not tell her of the trial. Instead they tell her of Leach's escape. Tell her of how he had hidden himself in the alleys of Polruan and vanished into the hills. Evaded capture.

"Evaded capture?" Flora repeats.

"Yes. I'm sorry, Mrs Kelly. We're doing everything we can to find him."

"Does he know I was the one who turned him in?"

"No. But I suggest you be watchful nonetheless."

She nods, strangely unaffected by the news. She isn't afraid of Tom Leach, she realises, because he is afraid of her.

When the riding officers are gone, she unwinds the strapping around the gash on her wrist. The cut is pink and raw, but healing well beneath the poultice of ground ivy. It will leave her with a scar, but it will be one that reminds her that she need not be afraid. Leach believes her inn is filled with black magic. Play up such a thing and he will never again venture through the door. Besides, she thinks, he has no way of knowing she was the one who had turned him in. His suspicions will go elsewhere.

Isaac, Flora realises, is the one who needs to be watchful.

She goes to the street, locking the door behind her and cocooning Bessie in the inn.

Candlelight flickers in the window of Isaac's cottage. She feels a strange flush of nerves as she knocks on the door.

Adulterer.

Intruder.

He looks surprised to see her. Despite the late hour, he is still dressed in his breeches and boots. His lips part, as though debating whether to invite her inside. Flora stays planted in the doorway.

"Leach is on the run," she says, before he can speak. "The riding officers went for him this afternoon. He got away."

He frowns. "What? How could they let such a thing happen? After you—"

Flora fixes him with hard eyes.

Don't.

She can't bear to hear the truth of it spoken.

Caroline appears from the bedroom, tugging a shawl around her shoulders. She is barefoot in her nightshift, her hair in a long plait down her back. Flora can't look at her.

"You and Bess ought to stay with us," Isaac tells her. "You're not safe in the inn."

She holds back an incredulous laugh. What is he thinking? "Leach doesn't know it was me who turned him in. He's far more likely to blame you. I came to warn you."

"She's right," says Caroline. "You're the one he'll suspect, Isaac. And it seems he would have had no issue with killing you in Lansallos." A tremor runs through her voice.

She and Caroline fear the same thing, Flora realises. They are both terrified of losing Isaac to Leach's bullet. And these, she thinks, are fears she has no right to have. These fears ought to be Caroline's alone.

Isaac glances between them. He must know, of course, that they share these unspoken thoughts.

Flora tries to catch his eye. She wants reassurance from him. Wants him to tell her that he will be safe and careful and that she need not fear losing him. But these fears, of course, are for Caroline, not her.

Isaac touches his wife's shoulder.

"I've got to go," Flora says hurriedly. "I left Bessie alone. I just thought you ought to know…"

As she is walking back to the inn, she hears him call after her.

She whirls around. "Go back inside. Caroline is no fool. She'll suspect something."

He reaches for her arm. "Please don't go back to the inn," he says breathlessly. "I hate the thought of you and Bess alone in that place."

She keeps striding down the hill. "Bess and I are just fine."

"Leach has come after you before."

"I'm not afraid of Leach."

"How can you say that after what he did to you on the beach?"

"That's exactly why I'm not afraid of him. He believes me a witch. He's too scared to come near me."

"Stay with us," Isaac says again. "You and Bess can take Scarlett's room."

She gives a cold laugh. "You can't be serious."

"Caroline doesn't know a thing. No one does."

Flora exhales sharply. She unlocks the front door. Isaac follows her inside. He grabs her waist and pulls her to him. Their faces are cold from a night on the edge of winter. He kisses her impulsively.

Flora tenses. She wants nothing more than to take him upstairs to that sanctuary at the top of the inn and feel his body against hers. She wants to lie in that thick dark and hear his breath in her ear. Wants to lie in his arms and feel the warmth of him. And then, she thinks, then she would finally sleep.

But she would wake and the rest of the world would come charging back. There would be Caroline and Leach and guilt and *adulterer.*

She turns away. "Stop. I can't. This isn't right, Isaac. I can't walk past your family in the street. I can't look Caroline in the eye. And what if the village were to find out about us? I've already had them turn on me once."

"I'd make sure everyone knew it wasn't your doing."

"It's always the woman's doing," she says bitterly.

Isaac runs his fingers down her cheek. "I can't just walk away and leave you here. Not with Leach on the run."

"I'm not afraid of Leach," she says again.

"You ought to be."

Sudden anger wells up inside her. "No," she says sharply, "you cannot tell me how I am to feel. What I ought to think. You cannot force me into acting the way you wish!"

Isaac frowns. "What are you—"

"Were you in on Reuben's lie?" she demands. "Was it your idea to have him tell me I'd be taken to trial outside of Cornwall?"

He rubs his eyes. "How did you know?"

"Does it matter?"

He begins to pace, hands folded behind his head. "I had to do something! You were going to face incarceration. And for what? To protect Leach against conviction for murders I saw him commit!"

"It was my decision to make, Isaac! How dare you try and manipulate me! And to work with Reuben, of all people!"

"Ayes, I was willing to work with Reuben. Does that not tell you how desperate I was to protect you?"

"I don't need your protection," she hisses.

He shakes his head in frustration. "Why can't you accept help? Even from me?"

"Because I don't want you to look at me with pity. I don't want to be that poor, helpless widow who can't save herself."

"Is that truly how you think I see you?" Isaac exhales sharply. "You're infuriating. You're so damn infuriating. I don't pity you, Flora. You're not the kind of woman who needs pity. The way I feel about you, I—"

"No," she says abruptly. "You can't say it. You can't." He cannot speak of love, then vanish across the ocean with his wife. She lowers her eyes, her heart pounding and her skin hot. "Please," she says throatily. "Just go."

Isaac's breath is hot against her ear. "You want this like I do. I know it."

"Yes. I do. But we cannot have it." She looks down. "Go back to your family. You've plans to make. Plans that are far more important now Leach has escaped."

She wants him on a boat out of Talland as quickly as possible. Wants he and his family gone. Yes, there will be an ache in her chest when she walks past his empty house, but it will be far easier than walking past he and Caroline in the street. "You need to leave," she tells him. "I'm sorry."

His footsteps sigh across the flagstones. The door closes with a creak and thud. Flora feels something sink inside her.

She goes upstairs to her mother's chest and reaches to the bottom for the bundle of cloth. She takes it out carefully and unwraps a globe of dark green glass. The watch ball. She lifts it by its rope hanger and watches it glow in the light of her candle. The ball had hung above the front door when she was a child. Protection against evil spirits.

She carries it downstairs to the bar. The hook on which it had once hung is still there, cobwebbed and rusting above the front door. She hangs it, then steps back to watch it sway in the draughty tavern. There is something calming about seeing it back where it had once been.

Who had taken it down? She does not remember. Her father? Her husband?

Had she removed it herself?

Who had decided the Mariner's Arms no longer needed protecting from evil spirits?

Evil spirits? Perhaps she believes. But she knows Leach will look at such a thing and see black magic swinging on a rope. Knows the sight of such a thing will prevent him from setting foot in her inn.

And the rest of the village? Will they look at her and see the village charmer? Come to her for magic rhymes and potions against the dark?

So be it.

The thought of it begins to dull the ache left by Isaac.

She will be *witch*.

But she will not be *adulterer*.

She runs a finger over the cloudy glass of the watch ball.
Goes back to the kitchen to finish the lambswool.

SECRETS

Asher is restless and sick as the coach rattles towards Talland. He doesn't want Caroline to see him like this. His shirt is a patchwork of stains and stenches, his skin discoloured with grime. She is supposed to look at him and see greatness. Not this miserable excuse for a man.

He knows the way it will play out. Caroline's eyes will flare and harden when she sees him, as they had the day he had walked into that cottage behind Scarlett. There will be bitter words and empty threats and she will tell him he has no place in her life.

He had had no place, perhaps, in the miserable grind she had built with Isaac, but Asher is returning with news that will upturn her world. This time he is returning with Jacob Bailey. The wall she has built around her secrets is trembling on its foundations.

Asher had first heard of Henry Avery's haul on a smuggling voyage to Guernsey. Had heard of the riches from Albert Davey, the man Jacob would gun down on the landing beach so he might get his hands to a little of the lost silver.

The moment Davey had spoken of the wealth, the path to Asher's dream life had begun to reveal itself. At last he would have a way of making it to university. A way of becoming a surgeon. Of becoming a great, respected man. At last, he would have a way of becoming better than the rest.

He and Jacob sat together in the tavern and made plans to uncover the haul. Their ideas were underhand and immoral, Asher knew, but immorality was a small price to pay in exchange for greatness.

The plans were kept a secret, of course, from everyone but the woman he loved.

He and Caroline had never spoken of their feelings, but Asher's love burned hot and sure. He wanted to wake every day beside her, ensconced in a lavish curtained bed. But he feared her feelings for him did not burn as brightly. How could he expect otherwise when he filled his days hauling fishing nets and came home smelling of bilge water?

Hearing his plans would change everything. He would tell her of the places his brilliant mind would take him, tell her of the lavish life he had planned. And she would come to love him as he loved her.

He was hot with desire as he climbed the stairs to her room. Tonight, she would see beyond his fishing boots and oiled coat to the man he truly was.

When she opened the door, he slid a hand around her waist and pressed his lips to hers.

She put an arm out, preventing him from entering her room. "If I were to let you in, what would I have to offer my husband?" No anger in her voice. Just challenge.

Asher returned her faint smile. "What does a man have to do to become your husband?"

"Are you asking for my hand?"

His heart pounded. "Do you wish it?"

Caroline tilted her head, her eyes glittering in the lamplight. "I'm yet to be convinced by you."

"Let me inside," said Asher. "There's a secret I wish to share with you."

Caroline gave a short laugh. "Does that line work for you often?"

His eyes hardened. "Trust me. You will want to hear this. This is what will convince you that I am worthy of your hand."

And so she lowered her arm. Let him inside.

They sat on the floor by the hearth with glasses in their hands and legs intertwined. In the flickering light, he told her of Avery's lost wealth. Told her of his crewmate who had produced a piece of silver from his pocket the night their ship was becalmed in the Channel. Told her of his plans to find the haul and the glittering life he would make for them.

He'd marry her then, Asher said. Then and only then, so she might be wed to a respectable surgeon and not a sea-stained pauper.

Instead of the smile Asher had been expecting, Caroline frowned. "You've no idea how to find this silver. You've not a thing to go on but the ravings of an old man. This is a just a child's treasure hunt." Firelight made the brandy in her glass glow the colour of autumn leaves. "I thought you more intelligent than that."

"It's far more than a child's treasure hunt," Asher hissed. "It's real. And we will find it. The old man, Davey, he has no need for it."

"We? Who is *we*? You and I?"

"The man's name is Jacob. We make the Guernsey runs together. He has means to get the information from Davey. He's promised me a share of the fortune if I help him."

"Means? He will threaten the man into telling him?" Her voice was even and controlled. Was she angry? Critical? Intrigued? Asher couldn't tell. He hated that he couldn't read her.

She sat with her back against the foot of the bed, staring into the fire. The dance of the flames accentuated the fine curves of her cheekbones. A ghost of a smile appeared on her lips. Asher knelt over her suddenly.

"I need to find this money," he said fervently. "I need to be far more than a lowly fisherman. I need to learn. To study. I'm destined for so much more than this, Callie. I've always known it. You know it too. You'd not be here otherwise." He pushed a dark strand of hair behind her ear. "I've never had a way to get there before. But now I do. I'm going to make a great life for myself. For us. You'll want for nothing."

Caroline smiled faintly. Asher had known he would have to work hard to make her see their future. But she had caught a faint glimpse of it. He could tell by the shine in her eyes.

"A fine house in London," he said, seizing the momentum. "A lady's maid of your own. Roast lamb for supper. Silk skirts and lace bonnets."

She raised her neat eyebrows. "These are quite some promises. I'm not entirely sure you can deliver."

Asher dove forward and kissed her. Tasted brandy on her tongue. "I can deliver," he said, full of certainty. "You'll have all those things. And everything else you desire. We'll have the life we have always wanted."

The carriage reaches Polperro.

Asher and Jacob begin the walk towards Talland; a silent march across the cliffs in which time falls away. Jacob makes for the landing beach. A cold irony, Asher thinks, for the man to lead him to this place.

Jacob presses his back against the jagged shards of rock on the edge of the beach. Asher remembers hiding in the same place, the night he had been wrecked. He can still see the dark bones of his ship beneath the surface.

Jacob's eyes are glassy. He has not been here for sixteen years. What is he thinking? Is he seeing his children build castles on the sand? Or watching Albert Davey's blood stain the thin thread of the river?

"Bring her here." His voice is thin, but dark with theat.

Asher nods. Begins to walk towards the cottage.

What is he doing, taking Caroline to this man? Can he truly trust him not to put a bullet in her chest? Not to put a bullet in his own chest?

He could run now. Run back over the cliffs towards Polperro and turn the Baileys in for smuggling. But do that and he will lose Caroline forever. His only chance of being with her is to take her to Jacob. Convince her to escape the past by rebuilding her life with him. Building that life they had dreamed of as they'd sat drinking brandy by the fire so many years ago.

He knocks on her door. His heart is speeding. He watches a look of horror fall over her face as she answers. She takes in the stains on his clothing, the bruises he can feel swelling at his cheekbones.

"What do you want?" she hisses. A stained apron is knotted around her waist, the skirts beneath it a misery of grey and white patching. She looks past Asher into the street. "Where's Scarlett?"

"I've no idea."

"She's not with you?"

"No. But—"

"Get away from my house." The door swings towards him.

"Caroline—" He puts a hand out, stopping the door from closing. "You need to come with me."

He sees a flicker of pity in her eyes which stings more than her anger. "What happened to you?"

He reaches for her arm, the tightness of his grip preventing her from pulling away. "Callie, listen to me." He looks into her eyes, trying to find that shrewd girl of seventeen. He sees only ice. "You need to come. Jacob is in Talland."

THE LIFE WE HAVE ALWAYS WANTED

The life we have always wanted, he said. Over and over; *the life we have always wanted.* Caroline had no idea what the life she had always wanted looked like. She had never allowed herself to dream.

She had not known her mother. Her father was dead before her fifteenth birthday. But Caroline considered herself luckier than so many of her fellow Londoners. She had a good job as a lady's maid, food on her table and a roof over her head. Alone, yes, but what did *alone* matter, as long as she was alive?

Her mistress, a bent and withered woman of seventy, had a weakness in her heart. *The sea air,* her doctor said. And so it was. The household would move to Cornwall, where the sea worked its way into everything.

To Caroline, the west country was so distant it may as well have been another land. But what was keeping her in London beyond her parents' graves? Cornwall was a distant land, but it was one with work. Security. Perhaps a future.

When the old woman died before a year was through, Caroline found the place had worked its way beneath her skin. She took a job as a wealthy couple's daily and found a room above the Three Pilchards. A room on the other side of the corridor from Matthew Fielding, the man who would come to call himself Asher Hales.

It was curiosity that drew her towards him. He was a fisherman— she had seen him return with the fleet many times— but he walked with his shoulders back and his chin lifted, as though he were a man of status. He drank red wine instead of mahogany. Spoke of medical advancements and the merits of slavery, refusing to acknowledge the superstitious garble coming from the local men around him.

He told her of foreign silver hauled from a recent pirate raid. She would have assumed it a myth had it come from anyone else. And he began to convince her that the life she had always wanted was a life of luxury at his side, paid for with stolen riches.

She had never known love. She supposed this was it. Matthew Fielding made her mind travel to new places and her body heat. Yes, love.

The soldiers came to the Three Pilchards early in the morning. A murder on the beach in Talland, they said. A dragoon had been assaulted. A young man in custody.

Her young man.

She couldn't bring herself to sit through his trial. Didn't know why. Was she too distraught? Perhaps. Or perhaps she wanted to distance herself from the whole affair.

The man she told herself she loved had sliced open the arm of a British soldier as he was hauled away from Albert Davey's dying body. Of the assault, he had little choice but to plead guilty. But he took no responsibility for Davey's murder.

Caroline was unsure whether to believe him. She knew Albert Davey held the secrets of Henry Avery's lost wealth. She knew there was every chance the jury would find Mathew Fielding guilty of murder. And if that happened, she did not want the crowd to look across the courtroom at her and see the woman who had talked herself into loving a killer.

She sat outside the courthouse and listened as the verdict spilled out of gossiping mouths.

Innocent of murder.

Guilty of assault.

Matthew Fielding would be spared the hangman but would spend the next decade a prisoner.

Caroline felt nothing.

The news came that he had been purchased by a land owner in the colonies. He would be shipped off to New England to serve his sentence as an indentured servant. A season's journey away.

The day before he was due to leave, she ventured to the prison at Launceston Castle. She walked the stone steps down to the jail, her skirts in her fist and her heart drumming. The stench of sweat and waste rose up to meet her, tightening her throat and turning her stomach. Her shoes clicked loudly against stone, announcing her arrival. She tried to tiptoe. Already, she regretted coming.

Five pairs of eyes turned to look at her as she approached the cell. Men mumbled, called, cursed. Matthew hissed at them to be silent. He stepped up to the bars. His hair hung loose on his shoulders, his chin patchy with the beginnings of a beard. Behind his eyes, she saw a new intensity. The darkness of them made her wary.

Caroline looked down. She knew that after she left the castle, she would never see him again. For the best, yes, she knew, but she did not want this wild-eyed creature to be the way she remembered him. Perhaps what she felt for him had not been love, but it had been as close as she had ever known.

He reached through the bars and lifted her chin, forcing her to look at him. "This is Jacob's doing," he hissed. "All of it."

Caroline thought to argue. Matthew Fielding had been convicted of assault. Surely no one's fault but his own. She said nothing. If he needed to blame another, let him.

"Jacob needs to be punished. I need you to make sure there's some sense of justice in this miserable world." His eyes glowed. Caroline could tell he had spent his days in the castle planning, plotting.

She knew him well. Knew he would do all he could do avoid conflict, but would plan and manipulate from dark corners. Spread trouble anonymously.

"Jacob has ruined my life," he said. "We need to ruin his."

He told her of his plan, detailed and precise. A plan she would carry out while he was tossed about by the sea and carried to another world.

No, she thought to say. *I'll not be a part of this. I'll not be a part of your revenge.*

But there was something about this man; something about the unsteady blaze in his eyes, the way he still held his chin high, even though he was dressed in rags. Something that made Caroline listen to every word of his plan, even though she knew she was being manipulated.

He looked her in the eye and said: "I know you'll do this for me. I'm all you have in the world."

Some logical part of her knew this was not true. Take Matthew Fielding out of her life and she was left with friends, work, home and a far simpler existence. But with his prison-hardened eyes on hers, she saw only loneliness. She saw empty nights alone in her room, countless hours of scrubbing dishes as she tried to scratch together a living. Saw a loveless life of spinsterhood now the man who wanted to marry her was to be shipped across the world.

"Yes," she said. "You are all I have in the world."

"We are to be torn apart by this man. Do you not want to see him punished?"

Caroline said: "Of course."

First, she was to seek out a man from Jacob's smuggling crew. A man who showed his captain no loyalty. An easy thing to find, Matthew had assured her. Jacob had near killed his crew two years earlier, overloading their ship on account of his greed and rolling it in the middle of the Channel.

"Edward Baker," Matthew said. "He has a wife and son in Talland. They say Edward fought with Jacob about overloading the ship. Edward told him it was dangerous, but Jacob pulled rank. Took the ship out anyway and near killed all his men. Edward's had a hatred for his captain ever since."

Caroline asked after Baker the next night at the tavern. The fishing boats had returned from sea and the inn overflowed.

"I hear you want rid of your captain." She had dressed in her best yellow skirts and pinned flowers in her hair in place of a cap. Ordered wine instead of her usual mahogany. She wasn't sure why. Was she trying to seem less of a troublemaker?

Edward Baker looked her up and down. "You're right," he said finally, curiously. "I don't trust my captain an inch. We'll all end up dead if we're to keep sailing with him." He shoved a pipe between his teeth. "How do you know these things? Who are you?"

Caroline was afraid the man might turn away when she mentioned Matthew Fielding's name, but he just grunted and blew a line of smoke at her. "I'm listening, girl," he said. "Whatever you got to say, I'm listening."

She tossed back a mouthful of wine to steel herself. "You want Jacob out of Talland. Out of your lives."

"Ayes. The man's a murderer. No doubt in my mind who killed poor Mr Davey. And I nearly died on account of Jacob's greed."

"I want him gone too. He ruined the life of the man I love."

There was a crooked smile in the corner of Edward's mouth. Caroline could tell he was yet to take her seriously.

"And how exactly do you plan to be rid of him?" he asked, a flicker of humour in his voice.

"He has a family."

"Ayes. A wife. Young daughter."

"And he would put their safety and happiness before his own?"

Edward lowered his pipe. "What are you suggesting?"

Caroline's hand tensed around the stem of her glass. It was not just about avenging Matthew anymore. It was about showing Edward Baker she was serious. Proving she was more than just talk. "Where can I find Jacob's wife?"

Edward tapped a finger against his bristly chin, considering her. Finally, he said: "The pilchard palace. Meet me by the harbour tomorrow afternoon and I'll show you who she is."

Jacob's wife was a slightly built woman who Caroline guessed could be no older than forty. Her striped blue skirts were faded beneath a grimy apron, a bulk of black hair knotted at her neck. She walked along the harbour with one of the other women, fish baskets clamped to their hips and their free hands flying in animated conversation. Jacob's wife tossed back her head and laughed, her dark eyes alight and warm.

Caroline watched from the other side of the harbour. Her stomach turned over. She wouldn't hurt the woman, she reminded herself. Not as long as Jacob did as he was told.

"She works here every day," said Edward. "In the afternoon, she collects her daughter from the charity school and they walk the cliff path back to Talland."

Caroline swallowed. "How old is the daughter?"

"A little one. Four, perhaps five."

She squeezed her eyes closed.

"Wait a while and she'll go for her. You'll see her."

"I don't need to see the girl," Caroline said hurriedly. She turned away, unable to watch Jacob's wife any longer. "The rest of the crew," she said, trying to force confidence into her words, "can we expect their loyalty? Or will they support Jacob?"

"I don't know," Edward admitted. "But it don't matter. Best we keep this whole business to ourselves in case there

are men in the crew still loyal to their captain. Jacob don't
need to know it's only the two of us involved. We'll tell him
we have the rest of the men on side. He'll have no way of
knowing us lying."

The following night, they went to The Three Pilchards for
Jacob. Edward nodded towards a man sitting alone at the
bar. He wore a blue knitted cap and dirty hide coat, his hands
wrapped around a tankard. Caroline watched him from the
doorway.

What had she been expecting? A burly, tattooed monster
with black eyes and sharp teeth? This was just a man.

She imagined him on the beach with a pistol in his hand.
Imagined him pressing his crewmate for information on the
lost silver. Imagined him pulling the trigger and leaving
Matthew alone on the beach with the bleeding body at his
feet.

Good. Now this was easier.

Caroline slid onto the stool beside him, Edward hovering
at her shoulder.

Jacob peered at her. A shag of grey streaked hair hung
over one eye. "Who are you?"

"I'm the woman who loves Matthew Fielding."

He shifted uncomfortably, then managed a faint smile.
"You're better off without him, maid."

"You've destroyed his life," she said. "And mine."

Jacob snorted into his ale. "The man was convicted of
assault. How is such a thing my doing?"

Caroline narrowed her eyes. The man's dismissiveness
made her neck prickle with anger. The harder she looked at
him, the easier it was to imagine him with a murder weapon

in his hand. For the first time since she had left Matthew in the castle, she began to believe she was doing the right thing.

"Go home, girl," said Jacob. "Get yourself a good night's sleep and you'll soon forget the bastard."

Anger flared inside her. She slid from her stool and stood close. "You destroyed our lives," she hissed. "And so we will destroy yours."

He chuckled. "You will, ayes? How will you do that?"

There again; that doubt. That flippant look in a man's eyes that said she was nothing but a triviality. "Your wife and daughter walk the cliff path back to Talland each afternoon," she said icily. "They make themselves easy targets up there in the open."

Jacob's eyes flashed. Something in them sent a shiver through her. Yes, she thought, Matthew was right. This man needed to be punished. And she had his attention.

"You will leave this place," she told him. "Tonight. You will be alone, just as Matthew Fielding is. And if you don't, we'll be waiting for your family the next time they try and cross the cliffs."

Jacob snorted. "You think I'd leave my wife and child on the empty threats of some jilted girl?" She heard the waver of uncertainty in his voice. Was buoyed by it.

"You think these empty threats? You took the man I love away from me."

"Matthew Fielding committed his own crimes. I had nothing to do with it."

"You left him on the beach with the man you killed!"

Jacob sucked in his breath at her raised voice. He glanced hurriedly around the noisy tavern. Caroline didn't take her eyes from his.

Jacob slid from his stool and stood close to her. He stank of sweat and sea. "Go near my wife and daughter and I will kill you."

"Kill her," said Edward, "and your crew won't let you live."

Jacob looked at him for the first time. Colour was rising in his cheeks. Caroline saw his fist clench around his tankard. "Ten years as your captain and this is what I get in return?"

"Do you truly expect loyalty? You near killed us all when you lost Reuben's cutter. And now our crewmate turns up murdered on the beach?"

"I didn't kill that man," Jacob hissed.

"We're not fools," Edward said blackly. "If you were willing to kill Davey, how do we know you'd not do the same to us? You'll leave. And you'll not come back. Leave our lives. Leave the syndicate. And if you even think of returning, know your crew will be watching for you. Watching for your wife and daughter when they make their way back along those cliffs."

Jacob clenched his jaw until it shook. "You're lying."

"Can you be sure of that?"

Jacob lurched suddenly at Edward. The two men clattered into the table, the tankard of ale splattering over the floor. Caroline stumbled backwards, pulling a knife from her pocket. She held it close to Jacob's chest. The feel of it in her hand made sickness rise in her throat. But the thing was almost done. She could not let him see her uncertainty now. Her fist tightened around the handle. "You know what you need to do."

Jacob gripped the edge of the table. His breath was hard and fast. "Let me see them one last time," he said finally. "Let me leave in the morning."

The ache in his voice made Caroline look away. She wanted suddenly to tell him to stay. Tell him it was all a mistake. She had not loved Matthew Fielding enough for this. But things had gone too far.

"You'll leave in the morning," she said.

"What are you doing?" Edward hissed at her. "He bloody well leaves tonight."

Caroline couldn't look at him. "You'll leave in the morning," she told Jacob again. "You'll see your family one last time."

"We'll be watching your house," said Edward. "Making sure you and your family don't try and escape in the night. In the morning you'll take the dory out. Let them believe you drowned."

The next night, Caroline sat in her room and penned the letter.

Jacob has left Talland...

She wrote slowly, carefully. The writing came out looking like someone else's. Good. She didn't want to be this person. This bitter, lovelorn woman who mourned manipulative men and destroyed lives. Perhaps Jacob had been right about Matthew Fielding. With him gone, she felt none of the loneliness he had predicted. Just a dull sense of relief. Perhaps he was a man who could be forgotten. Perhaps the flickering thing Caroline had uninformedly called love could be left in the past.

She leant close to the page as the candle hissed and spat.

He left this place in his fishing boat, the village believing him drowned.

Matthew would want to know everything, of course. He would want to know of the way they had hunted down Jacob's wife at the pilchard palace and how Caroline had pulled a knife from her pocket to end it all. But she had no desire to spell out the details. Had no desire to go back there, to put to paper a record of the things she had done. And so, the briefest of letters. The bare facts.

Jacob gone. Punished.

She left the letter unsigned, unable to see her name scrawled at the bottom of such atrocities. She sent it to Matthew's uncle in Bristol, as he had instructed. He would send for it, he'd told her, the moment he returned to England.

A strange thing, Caroline thought, sending the letter away, knowing it would not be read for a decade or more. By then, this whole sorry business would be a distant memory. If Matthew wanted to hunt down that phantom treasure, let him. But she would not let it consume her the way it had consumed him.

The life she had always wanted was hazy. She only knew it wasn't this.

"You're lying," Caroline tells Asher. "Jacob wouldn't dare come back." She hears the thinness of her voice, the desperation in her words. She has always been terrified that he might one day return.

"I'm not lying," says Asher.

She shoves hard against his chest, knocking him into the doorframe. "You went looking for him," she hisses. "You went looking for him because you still believe in that fairy tale of a treasure hunt."

He reaches a grimy hand towards her shoulder. His face is discoloured with bruising, his lip split and swollen. Does he truly mean to comfort her? She pushes his hand away. "I hoped your time in New England would be enough for you to forget all this."

"And forget you?"

"Yes." She doesn't look at him. "And forget me."

"I was not the one who went looking. It was Scarlett. I was an unwilling participant in the whole mess."

"You told Scarlett Jacob was alive?" Her legs feel suddenly weak beneath her. Her world is on the verge of toppling. "Does my husband know?"

"No," Asher says tautly. "Your husband doesn't know. But Jacob is quite desperate to speak with you. I suggest you come with me before he decides he would rather have words with his son."

Caroline goes to the cradle. Mary is clucking and kicking, her smock tangled at her waist. Her eyes light when she sees her mother. Caroline feels a sudden pain in her chest. There is so much Jacob could take from her. She feels trapped in the worst of her dreams.

She scoops Mary from the crib and places her in her basket. She follows Asher out of the cottage. The day is dark, threatening rain. Wind bends the trees and whips the sea into white peaks. Their footsteps crunch rhythmically. Where is he taking her?

"You call yourself a wise man," she tells him bitterly. "And yet you're still chasing this myth."

"You believed," Asher reminds her.

"I was a fool. And barely more than a child. You're a sad, resentful man who has hung his desperate dreams on a fairy tale."

"Can you not see the same resentment in yourself?"

The truth of it makes something tighten in Caroline's chest.

"Not that I blame you, given the life Isaac Bailey has provided you with."

She laughs humourlessly. "You think the resentment in me is Isaac's doing? No. This is guilt. This is the pressure of hiding the truth of what we did from my family." Her voice catches as a sudden rush of tears tightens her throat. She forces them away. "None of this is Isaac's fault. I love him."

Asher looks over his shoulder and gives her a faint, infuriating smile. His battered lip is fat and purple. "I'm sure you did, once. What else would have led you to do such a foolish thing as marrying Jacob's son?"

She feels him trying to catch her eye. Doesn't let him. Revulsion swells inside her. How could she have done the things she had done out of love for this man? The revulsion twists into self-hatred.

"Did you know it at the time, Caroline? Did you know who you were marrying? Did you know who his father was?"

"Of course not," she hisses. "I didn't even know Jacob had a son."

Isaac Bailey was everything Matthew Fielding was not. Isaac was honest, upfront. He had told her of his debt to Reuben the day they had met. A brutal thing, of course, but somehow, the fact that he had been so open about it had made it easier to carry.

The day she'd met Isaac in the Ship Inn, he'd been standing at the bar in his fishing boots, his hair windswept and his skin smelling of the sea. He was living the simple fisherman's life Matthew Fielding had been so desperate to escape. But a simple fisherman's life, Caroline had realised as they sat together in the inn, their knees edging closer to each other's, was all she needed. The day she met Isaac, the need for silk and satin Matthew had planted within her had fallen away.

Matthew Fielding's proposal at her bedroom door had been desperate and needy, full of plots and plans and empty promises. When Isaac had asked for her hand, there had been no talk of wealth, or luxury. But nor had she had any doubts. The joy of it was enough to push Matthew to the back of her mind and take Jacob with him. She was sure she would never see either of them again.

Her new husband rarely spoke of his father. There had been little love between them, Caroline could tell.

The father, the man responsible for the smuggling runs and the strain. A nameless, long dead man she knew no more of. Cared to know no more of. Isaac's father had piled them with debt. His memory had little place in their lives.

It had been no great revelation. No plate-smashing, gasping realisation on Caroline's part. In casual supper-time conversation, the father had been named— *Jacob*.

She sat at the table, letting the pieces float their way together.

Jacob who had died at sea.

Gone without a trace.

Her breathing quickened as she looked across the table at Scarlett.

Jacob with the young daughter.

Caroline excused herself and rushed to the bedroom. She lay on top of the bedclothes, her head swimming and her skin hot.

She thought of running. But Isaac's child was stirring inside her. And he had also stirred within her a love far deeper than the miserable flicker she had felt for Matthew Fielding. Life as Isaac's wife had brought her far more joy than the games she'd played chasing chests of buried silver.

She closed her eyes and tried to breathe. Edward Baker had died less than a year after they had sent Jacob away. No one else in the village knew what they had done. She could bury the past. Forget. Make it as though it had never happened. Never think of it and never think of it and never think of it until it was over and forgotten and gone.

Isaac came to the bedroom. Found her on her back, staring at the ceiling. He leant over her. Touched her forehead, her cheek, the swell of her stomach.

She caught the laces of his shirt and tugged him into a kiss. She would bury her secrets deep. Push that dark shadow of her past away.

For years she has tried to forget. Tried to believe what Isaac and Scarlett believe; that Jacob is dead and gone. She had convinced herself it was a likely possibility; an old man with no money, no family. It was likely that death would find him.

But there he stands, motionless on the landing beach, looking out across the sea he had disappeared on. Death has not found him.

Why has he dared return? He has seen through her empty threats, no doubt. But why now?

She realises then that he knows. Asher has told him the woman who had forced him to abandon his family is married to his son. She swallows, forcing away a violent wall of sickness.

She takes slow, careful steps towards him. Sets the baby's basket at her feet. Asher has disappeared. She is not surprised.

Coward.

She looks up at Jacob. She has never forgotten his face. And yet she had seen not a flicker of him in Isaac when she had met him in the Ship Inn. The resemblance is there, of course. It is there if you know to look. And never before has she known to look.

At the sight of Jacob, she is the pliable seventeen-year-old she had been the last time she had seen him, a wine glass in her fist to give her courage. She lifts Mary to her chest, needing her daughter's closeness. Her little hand is soft against her neck.

"Put her in the basket," Jacob says stiffly. "I can't look at her."

Caroline finds her voice. "She's your granddaughter."

"She's a reminder of my son's mistakes."

Caroline keeps the baby tight against her chest.

"Put her in the basket." Something in Jacob's voice chills her. She lays the baby in the carrier. Mary screeches in protest.

Jacob bends slowly, looming over the basket. He lowers his head until it is close to Mary's tear-stained face.

Caroline's heart thuds. "Get away from her."

Jacob tilts his head. "Do you think I will hurt her? Do you think I have it in me?"

"I don't know."

Mary shrieks louder and beats her fists into the air.

"I know you want to punish me," says Caroline. "But please don't hurt my child. I'm begging you."

Jacob gives a short laugh. "You've a nerve asking such a thing, after all you've done to my family."

"I would never have hurt Scarlett, I swear it."

Mary's tears stop momentarily as he presses a grimy finger to her chin. Her dark eyes widen.

"Asher Hales is just a sad, lonely man. But you have so much to lose. You're a fool to have stayed in this place."

"Please." Caroline's voice wavers. "Think of Isaac. She's his daughter."

Jacob stands. He is close; too close. Hot breath on her skin. His face is lined and weathered beneath the grey mess of his beard. "I often wondered if you were telling the truth," he says. "Whether you truly had my entire crew ready to kill for you if I dared come back. I could never have risked such a thing, of course. But I always dreamed of returning. Let the years pass and my crew forget. Or die. And then I would come back for Scarlett and Isaac. Free them from Charles Reuben." He watches the sea rise and fall. The ribs of the shipwreck poke between the dark peaks of water. "I was sure you'd no longer be here. And even if you were, I knew there'd be no one looking out for someone like you. I could put a bullet in your chest and there would be no one to stop me." He gives a short, humourless laugh. "And yet it seems the man looking out for you is my own son."

His words sound distant. Caroline hears her heart racing in her ears. Surely she is to die here on the landing beach in the shadow of Albert Davey. Jacob has dreamt of killing her for sixteen years and he will do it here, now, in front of her daughter. And then? And then he will go to Isaac and tell him everything. He will tell him the real reason he left his family and she will be dead and gone. She will have no way of ever telling her husband how deeply, desperately sorry she is.

She waits for the gun to appear.

Jacob stares her down. There is no gun.

Finally, she dares to ask: "What are you going to do to me?"

A crooked smile appears in the corner of his lips. She can see how much he is enjoying this game; toying with her while her baby wails at her feet. He reaches into his coat and Caroline stops breathing. But Jacob's hands stay in his pockets, as though he has a secret hidden in his fist.

He says: "I'm going to tell you where Henry Avery hid his haul."

HILLS OF SILVER

"Do you think me a fool?" Caroline says shakily. "You expect me to believe this? If the haul is where you say it is, why did you not claim it?"

"Do you really need to ask that?" Jacob tells her. "How could I have risked returning to Talland to uncover it? How could I have risked you and Edward Baker killing my wife and daughter?"

Hearing him speak the words is brutal. A reminder that, no matter how hard she has tried to forget, the past cannot be changed.

She is not a killer. Just the feel of that knife in her hand had made her skin prickle with sweat. She would never have raised a finger against Scarlett or her mother. But of course, Jacob had not known this. He had had no room for risk.

Caroline thinks of him bending over Mary's basket, his dirty finger pressed to her chin. No room for risk.

She wraps her arms around herself as icy wind tunnels in from the sea. "Why tell me this? Why me of all people?"

"I know when I left, my debts to Reuben were passed on to my son." Jacob laughs humourlessly. "What a difficult thing that must be for you."

The muscles in her shoulders tighten. She feels hot and sick. "So you'll tell me where the haul is hidden so we can pay off Reuben's debt?"

Jacob snorts. "No. I'm telling you where it is because I know there's a desperation in you to make your life better. That was what drew you to Matthew Fielding, ayes? Didn't he promise you a better life once he found that money? A life of wealth and luxury?"

Caroline stares at the colourless sand. She can't look at Jacob. Can't look at Mary, thrashing in the basket, begging to be held.

"I'm giving you a way to have that life you longed for." He takes a step towards her. Caroline shuffles backwards uncomfortably. "And yet what will happen if you go to your husband with an armful of foreign silver? He will ask questions. He will want to know how you found it. And you will be forced to admit to him what you did. Wife or no, do you really think Isaac will allow you to remain under his roof knowing all this?"

She lets out her breath. "And what of my children? Would you have them grow up motherless or would you have me take them from their father?"

"That is your decision." He glances down at Mary. "Truly, I care little what happens to those children."

Caroline plucks the baby from the basket and holds her tight against her chest. She smooths her hair until her tears begin to ease. "You are heartless," she tells Jacob, peering at him over the top of Mary's head.

"Do you truly expect otherwise after all you've put me through?"

"And do you truly expect me to believe this business about Avery's haul is not a trap?"

"It's not a trap. I want you out of my son's life. Away from my family. I'm offering you priceless information. Take the money. Have that comfortable life you've been denied."

"Without my husband."

"You've a marriage built on lies."

Caroline feels the ache of it in her chest. "So you will turn down your chance at that money for the good of your family."

"My need for that money has only ever been for the good of my family. I used to think what they needed most was for me to pay off my debts to Reuben. But it is far more pressing to get you away from Isaac."

"I love Isaac," she hisses. "And he loves me." But beneath her words, she feels a tug of doubt. "Why do this?" she asks. "Why not just kill me?"

Jacob folds his arms. "Because against his better judgement, my son chose to make you his wife. If I were to kill you, I would lose any chance of him ever allowing me back into his life." He sighs. "I know he'd not believe it if I simply told him what you did. He'll not believe a word that comes from me. Nor will my daughter. She thinks I abandoned her."

Caroline feels him trying to catch her eye.

"I know what you're thinking. You'll make up a lie about how you found the money." His voice drops. "It won't work. It will not be easy to get to. No one will ever believe you just stumbled upon it. Only a person who knows where to look would have any chance of finding it." He leans close. "A person who has been told a secret."

Caroline looks away uncomfortably. She knows he is right. "I don't want that money," she coughs. "I don't need it."

She thinks of Isaac's ankers hidden in the tunnel. Thinks of Leach's escape.

It is not safe for her family in Talland. Can Jacob tell *I don't need the money* is the biggest of lies?

They will find another way out. Isaac is on the road right now finding new buyers. She will not follow Jacob's directions towards what can be nothing but trouble.

She lays Mary back in the basket. "I'm sorry," she says, her voice thin. "I'm so sorry for everything. I would take it back if I could." She draws in her breath and meets his eyes. "But I will not do what you're asking. I cannot leave my family."

He grabs her shoulders and slams her hard against the rock. A cry of fear escapes her as pain jolts down her spine.

Jacob holds her against the cliff. "You'll do as I wish," he hisses. "You have too much to lose to disobey me." He shoots a glance at Mary.

"No," Caroline says shakily. "You're doing this for Isaac. You wouldn't hurt his child." She shakes her head. *You wouldn't, you wouldn't.*

"Can you be sure of that?"

She pulls her eyes from his.

"No. You can't. Just as I couldn't be sure you didn't have my entire crew on hand, ready to hunt down Scarlett." He keeps a firm hand against her shoulder, the rock cold and hard against her spine.

"This is how it feels," he hisses, the threads of his beard tickling her cheek. "This is what it's like to have no choice but to leave."

Caroline lets herself into the cottage. She lowers Mary's basket to the floor and her legs give way beneath her. A sudden, violent sob wells up inside her and echoes around the still house.

No choice but to leave.

Jacob had left the beach without saying more. Does he truly mean to come for Mary? If she stays in Talland, how long will it be before he breaks down the door and spills all her secrets? The uncertainty of it is terrifying.

Caroline looks over at the baby. She has fallen asleep in the basket, her chest rising and falling beneath the blanket. Her tiny lips are parted, long lashes dark against her pale skin. Caroline squeezes her eyes closed. It hurts too much to look at her.

She hears footsteps outside the house. She scrambles to her feet as Asher passes the window. There are few people she wants to see less, but he knows far too much about her past to let him slide off into the village.

She wipes her eyes hurriedly. Lets him inside before he knocks. "Where is Jacob?"

"I talked him out of asking for a room at the Mariner's Arms. Told him it was best he keep his distance. He's gone to Polperro to find a room at the Ship."

Caroline swallows heavily. The Ship Inn is a tavern populated by the fishing fleet. Would Isaac recognise his father if he stumbled across him in a crowded room?

She presses a hand to her mouth to stop another sob escaping.

Asher touches her shoulder. "Oh, Callie."

She shoves him away. "The smell of you turns my stomach. As does the sight of you."

Something passes across his eyes. "You know," he says after a moment.

She flinches. "Know what?"

"Have we not had enough of games?" He lifts his chin. "Jacob knows where Avery's haul is. And so do you."

"Avery's haul is a myth. That's all I know of it."

Asher smiles slightly. "You've always been a terrible liar. But a fine keeper of secrets."

She looks away.

His fingers slide around her elbow. "Jacob told me you know. Tell me where it is. We can have that life we dreamed of."

Caroline exhales sharply. "Do you honestly think that's what I want? I've made a life! One without you in it."

He waves an arm around the cottage, with its rickety table and threadbare curtains, the smoke-stained bricks above the fireplace. "This sorry life? This is what you have made? I could give you so much more than this."

She feels a sudden urge to strike him. "You cannot give me anything! You have nothing." She stands close to his beaten, discoloured face. "You are nothing."

She sees the faint quiver of his jaw. This is the way to break him down, she knows. Chip away at his fragile sense of self-worth.

"That is not true," he hisses. "You know it's not. I've a life of greatness ahead of me. I'll be a fine surgeon one day." And she is that foolish girl with brandy in her hand, leaning close to hear him blather about vast, unreachable dreams.

Listening to him plan out the details of the life she had always wanted.

"No," she spits. "No you won't. You'll never be anything more than the filthy, desperate fool you are now." She turns away, unable to look at him. The sight of Asher Hales reminds her of all the worst parts of herself.

He grabs her arm, yanking her towards him. His eyes are flashing. "Where is the money?"

Caroline lets out her breath. "Jacob told you I know where the haul is because he wants us to destroy each other. Can't you see that? He didn't need to tell me. Threatening my daughter would have been enough. But he wants this. He wants you and I tearing each other apart over money we will never get our hands to."

"Why will we not get our hands to it?" he demands. "Where is it?"

Caroline hesitates. If she tells him what she knows, will he take the money and leave without her? She can't be sure. Perhaps it's worth the risk.

She opens her mouth to speak, but something stops her. That money will get her family away from Reuben. Away from Tom Leach. It will bring them safety, security, a life without debt. If there is even a scrap of a chance she can get her hands to it without Isaac asking questions, she needs to try.

Asher digs his fingers into her bare forearm. "You know how long I've dreamt of finding that wealth," he hisses. "You know what it means to me."

"You think it will make you a good man. A worthy man. But you and I, we'll never be good or worthy. Look at what we did to Jacob's family."

"Jacob deserved all he got."

"Perhaps. But what about Isaac and Scarlett? What about their mother? Did they deserve it?"

"Love has made you soft," Asher says bitterly.

Caroline pulls her arm away. "Leave." She stares at the floor. In the basket beside her feet, Mary sighs in her sleep.

Caroline hears Asher breathe close to her ear. "I know everything about the Talland smuggling ring," he says finally. "And I will go to Customs House and tell them all of it. See Isaac and Scarlett in the hands of the authorities."

Caroline swallows heavily. Forces herself not to react.

"Or you will tell me where the haul is. And you will leave this place with me once we find it."

No. She will not let him trap her. Will not let him win. This man is smart. A plotter. Manipulator. But she can match him.

"Leave with you?" she repeats, her voice controlled and even. "Is that truly what you want?"

He presses grimy fingers to her cheek. Lifts a loose piece of hair from her face and tucks it behind her ear.

Chin lifted. Shoulders back.

Look at him, she thinks, bruised and bloodied, grappling at the shadow of the man he longs to be. The entire time she has known him, he has been lost in a dream.

When I become the man I am destined to be...

Their life would begin then.

You'll love me when I become the man I am destined to be.

Sixteen years later, he is still clinging to the same beliefs. She can see it in the desperate shine of his eyes. He will find the haul. He will become that great surgeon. And she will come to see he is a better man than her husband. She will see he is the man she ought to have chosen. The man she ought to love.

She sits at the table and clasps her hands. "I need time."

"How much time do you think you have? Jacob has been waiting to punish you for the past sixteen years."

Caroline swallows a wave of sickness. "I will bring the money to you tomorrow night," she says. "And we will leave."

His fingers run over the bare skin on the back of her neck. "Where is it hidden?"

She flinches. "You don't need to know. But I will have it for you."

"Tonight," he says.

"No. It's not enough time."

His voice hardens. "Tonight, or I tell customs of the smuggling tunnel. Of the false bottom on your husband's ship."

Caroline sucks in her breath. "I'll not go without my children."

"Very well. Bring them. Meet me at the Ship Inn. We will leave at midnight."

"No." Her memories of the Ship are of Isaac at the bar in his fishing boots. She will not have them tainted by Asher Hales. "I'll meet you at the harbour."

THE MAN WITH THE LOST DREAMS

The stream of customers into the Mariner's Arms is steady, despite the miserable emptiness of the liquor shelves. Flora wonders if the fishermen who charge in and toss back tankards of spiced ale are doing it purely in an act of solidarity towards her. Either way, she is grateful.

She is surprised when Isaac slips through the door. She doesn't want him in the inn. Doesn't want in the village. Just the sight of him makes her heart jump and ache. It will be far easier when he is gone. Far easier and far more difficult.

He leans against the bar, gives her apologetic eyes. "I'll not stay. I just wanted to make sure you were all right." His voice is low, secretive. The sound of it makes something stir inside her.

She gives him a small smile. "Everything is fine."

He nods at the watch ball swaying above the door. "Protection against evil spirits?"

"Or evil men."

"Do you truly think this will keep Leach away?" Curiosity in his voice, not criticism.

Flora concentrates on wiping the counter top, unable to look him in the eye. "Leach is a superstitious man. He fears magic. And he believes I can wield it."

"And you?" says Isaac. "Is that what you believe?"

She scrubs harder. "I believe I dismissed my mother's craft too quickly." The admission makes colour rise in her cheeks. She stops. Isaac is not the person to discuss such things with. He has seen too much of the world to give any weight to Cornish superstition. But she has also seen too much to cast it aside.

"This change in you," he says carefully, "it happened when we opened the tunnel. Are you thinking of Jack? Do you think he—"

"It's not about Jack," she says, too quickly. "Jack is gone. There's nothing more to it." She feels Isaac trying to catch her eye. Doesn't let him. "Besides," she says, "it doesn't matter what I believe. It matters what Leach believes. And I'm sure his fears will be enough to keep him away."

Isaac presses a hand to her wrist, forcing her to look at him. "I hope you're right."

He pulls his hand away as the door creaks.

Will Francis.

Isaac whirls around to face him. "What happened to John? Is he–"

"He's alive," says Will, sliding onto a stool at the bar. "Resting at home. Barber surgeon took the ball out. Managed to keep him alive."

Isaac exhales sharply. "Thank Christ." He claps Will on the shoulder. "You're a good man to have brought him back safely."

Will smiles at Flora. "It were your doing, Mrs Kelly. The yarrow you gave John kept him alive til we got to Plymouth."

His words fill her with a pride she had not been expecting. She fills two glasses of ale and places them on the bar. "Here. All I can offer, I'm afraid. But you'll drink to John nonetheless."

Will grins, tossing a mop of fair hair from his eyes. "Not hiding anything under the bar for us then?"

"Wouldn't dare. I've gotten to know the excisemen a little too well in your absence. Unless you want to climb into the tunnel and help yourself to Isaac's brandy, there's little I can do."

Isaac takes the glass and, finally, the stool at the bar. "I found a buyer in Bodmin," he tells them. "An innkeeper willing to take the rest of the brandy. Forty pounds for the lot."

Flora's eyebrows shoot up. "Forty pounds? That will give you enough to leave."

Isaac nods. He takes a long mouthful of ale, not looking at her.

She had wanted this, she reminds herself. Things will be easier once he is gone. Never mind the knot that has lodged itself in her stomach. She had wanted this.

"I'm glad for you," says Will. "That bastard Reuben will have to find someone else to make him his fortune."

"As am I," says Flora. Is her voice too bright? Too flat? Why is she having such trouble speaking normally? She squeezes her cloth between her fingers. Bends her head to catch his glance. "Tell your wife."

Isaac nods. "I will."

The cottage is quiet, the children asleep. Rain patters against the window.

Caroline can't handle the stillness. Stillness gives her too much room to think. She wants Isaac home, Mary fussing, Gabriel leaping about the house in mud-caked boots. And yet the thought of seeing any of them is a deep, unplaceable ache.

She paces. Finds herself gnawing a thumbnail; a nervous habit she had left behind in childhood.

They will leave tonight, she had told Asher. Told him words he had wanted to hear. Words that would get him out of her house, her life, however fleetingly. Words she had never intended to see through.

But perhaps it's best she truly does leave. Disappear from Isaac's life before he finds out what she has done. Agree to Asher's demands before he goes to the revenue men with everything he knows.

But what of the children? She can't bear to leave them. Can't bear to take them from their father. And the money? It would see her family far away from this place. See new clothes for her children, boots without holes. Nights without hunger and forced smuggling runs.

But Jacob is right, damn him to hell. Uncover those riches and she will face questions. There is no way she can claim to just have stumbled upon the money. Isaac will question and probe and her most dreadful of deeds will spill into the open.

The door clicks and creaks. She stops pacing as Isaac enters. She hovers awkwardly, gripping the edge of the table.

He frowns. "Are you all right?"

"Of course." Her heart is pounding. Can he see the secrets behind her eyes?

He comes towards her, a smile curling the edge of his lips. A buyer in Bodmin, he tells her. He will make the sale in two days' time. Forty pounds in their pocket. Enough to leave.

Caroline closes her eyes. This is the news she has longed for. How she wishes she could be happy. But there are mere hours before midnight and still she has no idea what she will tell Asher.

"I thought you'd be happier," says Isaac, hanging his damp coat over a chair.

She touches his cheek. "I am happy. You've done so well." He can he tell her smile is forced, she is sure. After twelve years together, they know every shift and nuance of each other's faces. Know how to read even the subtlest of expressions. But lately, they have also come to an unspoken agreement not to ask questions. A silent accord that their marriage will survive better if they keep their thoughts to themselves. He will come home late from the inn and she will ask nothing. She, harbour a fierce grudge against the man from the wreck and he will ask nothing. It is a brutal, lonely thing, but a thing Caroline is glad of now. If Isaac were to find out what she is hiding, she knows there would be a look on his face she had never seen before.

"Perhaps you might start to ready the house," he tells her. "Clear the shelves and the like…"

Ready the house.

Their escape is finally in reach.

To hell with the money. It doesn't matter. Leave the wealth to Jacob and Asher. Let them fight over it, destroy each other over it. She can live with holey boots, live with supperless nights. She will eat stale bread every day for the rest of her life if only she will be free of this place, safe with her husband and children.

She kisses Isaac impulsively. Tastes the rain on his lips. "Ready the house," she says. "Yes, I'll do that."

He smiles stiffly. "Will you come to bed?"

"In a while. I'm not tired."

He falls asleep quickly, his heavy breathing sounding beneath the bedroom door. Caroline sits by the dying fire. The last embers shift and crackle.

Less than an hour until midnight. Soon, Asher Hales will be waiting for her at the harbour.

And the answer comes. Manipulative. Underhand. What better way to trap such a man.

She goes to the bedroom. Hanging inside the wardrobe is Isaac's greatcoat, stained with John Baker's blood. She takes it back to the kitchen and slides on her cloak.

"Mammik?" She freezes at the sound of Gabriel's voice. His dark head appears around the door of the children's bedroom. "What are you doing?"

"Nothing, my darling. Just cleaning Tasik's coat." A tremor in her voice, though she knows, at eight years old, her boy is too young to think her words anything other than truth. Too young to believe his mother capable of lies and deceit. She doesn't deserve this unconditional trust.

He chews the sleeve of his nightshirt. "Why are you wearing your cloak?"

"I'm cold, is all." She kisses the side of his head. "Go back to bed."

She waits for his footsteps to patter back to the bedroom. Waits for silence.

The coat in her arms, she slips out of the cottage.

Asher is waiting at the edge of the harbour. He has washed his face and tied back his hair, but he wears the same dirt-encrusted shirt and breeches. The glow of the street lamps accentuates the bruises on his cheeks.

He eyes her. "Where are your children?"

"At home in bed." Caroline shivers, pulling Isaac's coat close to her body. A misting rain is cold against her cheeks. The sea clops against the harbour walls.

Asher looks down at the greatcoat. "What is that?"

She meets his eyes. "Your coat. Stained with the blood of the two riding officers murdered in Lansallos last week."

He glares. "That coat belongs to your husband."

"Can you prove that?"

"Prove it?" he snorts. "To who?"

"To the revenue men. The magistrate."

"What are you talking about?"

Caroline's heart is speeding. "You try and turn Isaac and Scarlett over to the revenue men and I will be right behind you with this. Evidence of your involvement in the riding officers' murders."

Asher's eyes flash. He opens his mouth to speak, but Caroline continues. She hears her voice grow stronger. "The revenue men have proven they're desperate to make an arrest. Make a point to other smuggling gangs. They care little whether or not they're convicting the right man."

Asher forces a cold laugh. "That will never work." Uncertainty in his voice. "You've nothing but your word."

"And your bloodstained coat. It's far more than Flora had to convict Tom Leach. And yet the authorities are more than willing to have her take the stand."

Asher's jaw tightens. Caroline feels a flicker of satisfaction. "You're a man with a criminal past," she says. "A man with an unsolved murder hanging about him. A fine suspect to pin a crime on." She clenches her fingers around the coat. There is something pleasant about reminding him of these things. Reminding him of how far he is from the man he longs to be. "Flora doesn't have it in her to lie before a court," she says. "When they catch Tom Leach, she'll crumble in the witness stand and the revenue men will have nothing. But you can be sure that I will have no difficulty standing before a jury and claiming I saw you return to our cottage the night of the murder, dressed in this."

For a long time, Asher says nothing. A peal of laughter rises from the Three Pilchards. "You are a manipulative witch."

Caroline smiles crookedly. "I must have learned such things from you."

She turns to leave. Asher grabs her arm. When she looks back at him, his steely façade has given way to desperation. "I have nothing," he hisses. "No money for food, or clothing. Nowhere to sleep. I lost everything I had when I was wrecked upon that cursed beach." He grips her cloak, pulling her close. "You have to help me." She turns her head, repulsed by the stink of him. "Give me a little of the money."

"I don't have the money," she says. "I don't care about it."

Asher pulls on the edges of her cloak. Fixes her with wild, glowing eyes. She has seen this look before. Seen it when he'd stood before her in Launceston Castle and told her of his plan to destroy Jacob Bailey. "You're planning to leave," he says suddenly.

She shakes her head. Asher can know nothing of her plans. She can't trust him not to tell Jacob.

"You are. I know it. You're not foolish enough to stay here and risk Jacob hurting your children." He pulls her close, his nose grazing hers. "You have a way out, don't you."

Caroline shoves him away and begins to walk back to Talland. She waits for him to follow, but there is nothing but stillness as she charges up the dark path. She is bristling with nervous energy. She pulls Isaac's coat tight against her chest to steady herself.

In the morning, she will ready the house. Pack the last twelve years into travelling trunks so they may start again.

Their way out is hazy and unformed. But they have no choice but to succeed.

Asher watches until the tiny figure of her is lost on the darkness of the hill. His legs give way beneath him. He sits at the edge of the harbour, hopelessness welling inside him. Water kicks up from the edge of the moorings, splashing his legs and stinging his eyes.

Caroline is right. His dreams of greatness will only ever be dreams. The realisation is brutal, vicious. He doesn't believe any more. He puts his head to his knees. What else is there to do?

"That was Isaac Bailey's wife," says a voice behind him.

Asher turns. Looks up. The man standing over him is tall and thin, his greatcoat dirty and far too large. His hair and beard are streaked with grey. Skin hangs in pockets beneath his eyes. Asher knows this man. Tom Leach, the trader with the black ship.

"What is she doing out here with you so late at night?"

"That's no business of yours."

Leach chuckles. "It's a sorry day when a woman brings you to your knees."

Asher turns away. He watches shadows move across the surface of the water. Somewhere in the darkness, a gull lets out a mournful cry.

Why is Leach here, Asher wonders distantly. If Caroline is to be believed, the witch in the inn had turned him in for murder. Why has he returned to Talland when the shadow of the scaffold hangs over him? Asher lets the thought peter out. He doesn't care.

"You're a sad and sorry man, aren't you," Leach chuckles.

"I'm a great man," Asher says flatly. "You've no idea of the things that await me."

"And yet here you are on your knees, staring desperately after another man's wife."

The truth of it is a deep ache within him. Asher Hales has never felt further from greatness.

"The Baileys are planning to leave?" asks Leach.

Asher nods faintly, not looking at him.

"That can't happen. Isaac Bailey does not just get to go free. Not when he's sent the authorities after me."

Asher thinks to tell Leach it was the witch who had condemned him. But no. Let him blame Isaac. He looks up at the dark figure standing over him. They are both sad and sorry men, Asher realises. He has far more in common with this outlaw than he does with the surgeons and scientists he longs to walk among.

Leach holds out a hand to haul Asher from the ground. "Tell me what you know."

WALKING IN THE DARK

The sky is white with morning light when Scarlett and Jamie reach Talland. From the top of the hill, the sea stretches out endlessly, a glassy lake after the heaving ocean on the north coast. Red and grey roof tops are speckled between the trees, the church spire a silhouette on the cliff.

Scarlett stays motionless, feeling the horse breathe beneath her. The view is achingly familiar. Everything has shifted, yet this place is constant, unchanging.

"I can walk the rest of the way," she tells Jamie. "There's no need to come down into the village."

His chest is pressed against her back, his arms reaching around her as he grips the reins. She has grown accustomed to the feel of it. She doesn't want to slide from the saddle and confront the real world. But the journey is over. She must face Isaac and Jamie must leave.

"I need to rest the horse before I return to Portreath." His voice is close to her ear.

"Will you make it back for the press gang's trial?" she asks.

"I hope so."

"What will happen to them? The hangman?"

"More likely, they'll be forced into the navy themselves."
She hears a smile in his voice. "It seems a just thing." He
dismounts and offers her a hand as she slides from the horse.
He keeps her fingers in his for a moment. "I'll find lodgings
in Polperro tonight. Come and see me in the morning. I'll not
leave until I've said goodbye."

Scarlett nods. Manages a faint smile. She doesn't want
goodbye. But brass-buttoned Jamie cannot stay.

He kisses her cheek. "Good luck."

She watches him leave. And she begins to walk down the
hill.

There is the cottage. Home, but it makes her stomach roll.

She will go inside and ask forgiveness for the distrust she
had had in Isaac. Forgiveness for running away. She will tell
her brother all she has discovered. She has come back to
Talland so she might do these things. But something stops
her. A sudden fear.

Perhaps Isaac will not forgive her for the things she had
said to him. Perhaps he will not forgive her for racing
unannounced into the world and upturning the lie they had
both known to be truth. Perhaps the door will be closed on
her and she will be forced to carry the knowledge of who
their father is alone.

And then what? She can't live a life without her brother
in it. Isaac has been more of a father to her than Jacob ever
was.

She keeps walking. Past the cottage. Through the
creaking gate of the churchyard. She weaves through the
crooked headstones until she stands among her family's
graves.

She kneels at her mother's headstone. Runs a finger across the weathered letters. Had her mother known the truth of who Jacob was? Had she seen something beneath his eyes that might have shown her the kind of man she had married? Or had she been blinded by love, the way Scarlett had been?

Beside her mother; two brothers. *Robert, Michael.* When Scarlett thinks of these names, she remembers hands lifting her high in the air, peals of boyish laughter. But perhaps these hands, this laughter belongs to Isaac. Her memories are faint and fragile.

Three that had been and gone before her time. Just names. *August, Elizabeth, Emily.*

And the memorial stone for her father.

It had made her happy, once, to think that Jacob was not down there in the earth with the others. That he might be freer than the black-eyed things the rest of her family had become.

She turns away. She can't bear to look at the memorial, tainting the resting place of her mother and siblings. She leaves the cemetery. She cannot go home. Not yet. She cannot face Isaac with such restlessness beneath her skin.

Someone is in the cellar. Someone earthly, real. Someone who has crawled into the tunnel from its mouth on the eastern beach.

Flora hears movement from behind the locked door, far too heavy to be mice. Far too solid to be the walking of the dead. The dog yaps and scrabbles against the door.

She takes a knife from behind the bar and slowly turns the key. The dog charges into the dark mass of the cellar. The morning light in the bar does little to light the shadows.

Flora lowers herself onto the top step, hearing it creak beneath her. She lights the lamp at the top of the staircase and slides it from its hook. The beam skims over broken furniture, ankers of ale, the barrels stacked across the mouth of the tunnel. Have they been moved? Impossible to tell.

The dog is weaving between the furniture, nose to the floor. He stops trotting. Pricks up his ears. There is silence now. Nothing but the irregular breath of the lantern flame.

Had she been wrong? The sounds had been so real. Perhaps she has spent too long staring into the black mirror. Is the line between this world and the next beginning to blur?

A knock at the front door startles her. She blows out the lamp and locks the cellar. Finds Scarlett on her doorstep.

Flora pulls her into a tight embrace. She is glad to see her. Glad she is safe. Glad for the steadying arms around her. With another person in the bar, her excursion to the cellar suddenly seems foolish. With another person in the bar, it is easy to blame her imagination.

She steps back, holding Scarlett at arm's length. "Where have you been?" she asks, in a faintly scolding voice usually reserved for Bessie.

Scarlett opens her mouth to speak. Says nothing. Her dark hair is windblown, her eyes large and sombre.

"You'll tell me when you're ready, ayes?"

Scarlett nods. "Can I come in?"

"Of course." Flora ushers her inside. She glances at the pack slung over Scarlett's shoulder. "You've not been home."

She shakes her head slightly.

"Isaac is worried for you," says Flora.

Scarlett squeezes her eyes closed. "I can't face him. Not yet. I said such terrible things to him. I'm so afraid he'll not forgive me."

Flora pulls her into her arms again. Is she trying to comfort Scarlett or herself? She can't be sure.

Tea. Yes. It will steady them both. She takes Scarlett's arm and walks with her upstairs.

Flora goes to the kitchen and hangs the kettle over the range. She hears the floorboards creak beneath Scarlett's feet. Hears her chatter with Bessie in the room full of flowers.

"Angelica," says Bessie. "Mallow leaves. Yarrow."

Flora finds them both at the window, staring down into the street.

"There's men here, Mammik." Bessie doesn't turn.

"It's Reuben," Scarlett says darkly. "And his footmen."

Flora puts the tea cups on the side table. A knock rattles the front door. A second knock without pause. The dog barks and scratches.

"Mrs Kelly?" calls Reuben. "Open the door please." There is a thinly-veiled anger in his voice Flora has not heard before.

She ushers Bessie towards her bedroom. "Reuben has been asking to see the tunnel," she tells Scarlett. "I told him it wasn't finished so Isaac could hide his brandy ankers in there. But I'm afraid he's come to see it himself."

"Brandy ankers?" Scarlett repeats. "Isaac made a run of his own?"

"Ayes. He means to leave as soon as he's sold them."

Scarlett sucks in her breath. "I need to see him."

Another thump on the door.

244

Scarlett hurries down the stairs. "I'll go to the tunnel," she tells Flora. "Hide the brandy on the beach."

Flora nods. Opens the cellar door for Scarlett and locks it behind her. She answers Reuben's fourth knock, giving him her warmest smile.

"The tunnel," he says darkly. "I hear it is finished."

Two footmen stand behind him. Their hair is windswept, dust streaking their coats. And Flora feels something tighten in her chest.

Footsteps in the tunnel. Footsteps in the cellar. Reuben had had his footmen sail around the point and enter the tunnel from the beach. Catch her in her lies.

"I wish to see it," he says.

"I'm afraid now is not a good time."

"Why not?" Reuben strides into the house, trailed by his men.

Flora feels a sudden surge of anger. "Surely these men do not need to charge into my home this way," she says, managing a little of her own sharpness. "This feels very threatening, Mr Reuben."

He hesitates. Finally, he nods. "Wait for me outside," he tells the men. The door slams as they leave. Reuben strides towards the cellar.

"I've just made a pot of tea," Flora says hurriedly. She can hear the strain in her voice. "Perhaps you would like a cup?"

Reuben nods at the cellar. "Unlock the door please."

If she refuses? Surely he will not hurt her. But her refusal will arouse his suspicion. She needs to take him down there. A slow, careful walk through the dark that might give Scarlett time to slide the ankers onto the beach.

She slides the key into the cellar door. In and out, in and out. She jiggles it in the lock. "I'm sorry. This door, it catches dreadfully." She glances at Reuben. Sees the thin smile on his face. She eases open the door and takes the lantern hanging at the top of the cellar stairs. She fumbles with the tinderbox and lights it carefully.

Had Reuben's men found the ankers when they had crept through the tunnel? And if they had, would they have had any thought as to what they were?

She leads Reuben into the passage. Takes slow, careful steps. And the light falls on the barrels of brandy sitting at a bend in the tunnel. Scarlett has managed to move less than half.

Flora tries to slide past them, hoping the ankers might hide themselves in the shadows. But Reuben stops walking.

"What are these?"

Flora hears Scarlett breathe in the darkness behind her.

"Are you hiding contraband?" Reuben demands.

"Of course not. They belong to me. I hid them after the excisemen found my licence."

"Do you think me a fool?" She has never heard Reuben raise his voice before. "I bought your liquor back from you not two days ago."

She holds the lamp close to his face, making him squint in the hot light. "And do you imagine you are the only man I conduct business with? Where would I be if the revenue men were to uncover your operation?"

He eyes her. "Who else did you buy from?"

"That's no business of yours."

Reuben snatches the lamp. He bends, shining the light over the surface of the barrels. He makes a noise from the back of his throat. "You're hiding contraband," he says again. "For who? Isaac Bailey?"

"You're mistaken."

He looks at her closely. The flickering light accentuates his deep frown. "I see," he says, but Flora can hear the disbelief in his voice. There is something else there too. Disappointment?

She can see this through his eyes. He has done nothing but support her since she had first spoken of opening the Mariner's Arms. And she has given him lies in return. His eyes are cold and unforgiving. Flora sees she can no longer count on protection from Charles Reuben. Can no longer count on his amnesty.

Silence hangs between them.

Reuben shifts his weight and Flora flinches.

He will not hurt her, surely. She tells herself again. *He will not hurt her.*

"I'd best go," he says finally, shortly. "My men are waiting."

Flora stiffens. Perhaps Reuben will not hurt her, but she knows his men will have no issue with such a thing. Reuben will direct them as a general directs his troops and they will obediently go after whichever fool has dared to cross him.

He begins to walk slowly from the tunnel, his footsteps crunching on the earth.

Scarlett presses her back hard against the wall, her face turned from the light in Reuben's hand. Finally, he and Flora are gone. Dark falls over the tunnel.

She has to get to Isaac. Tell him Reuben has found the brandy.

Trailing a hand along the wall to keep her bearings, she runs towards the thin shaft of light at the end of the tunnel. She clambers through the split in the rock and her boots sink into sand. The beach is hemmed by purple-black slate, the rock extending into the water like jagged walls. The only way back to the village is through the sea and around the point.

Gripping her skirts in her fist, Scarlett runs into the water. Waves swell around her waist, the current knocking her from her feet as the cold tightens around her lungs. The rocks are slippery beneath her boots. Barnacles tear the skin from her hands. Half-swimming, half-climbing, she scrambles around the point until she reaches the landing beach.

She hunches, exhausted, and squeezes the seawater from her skirts. Gulping down her breath, she hurries up the sand towards the cottage.

The door is locked. She rattles it, thumps loudly. "Isaac?"

Silence.

She knocks again. "Is anyone there?"

Moth wings patter against the glass. Scarlett hears her heart thudding in her ears.

She will not panic. Isaac is out fishing. Caroline has taken Gabriel to school.

No. Today is Friday. The charity school is closed.

She goes to the window. Peers through the murky glass into Isaac and Caroline's bedroom. The wardrobe door hangs open. Empty.

Her stomach knots.

The next window. The kitchen shelves are bare. Stray pots are strewn across the floor. Beside them, a trunk is overturned, clothes lying in a heap. Has someone else been here? Or have they just left in a hurry? She cannot tell. She only knows this is the house of people who do not plan to return.

She shivers in her wet clothes.

Had Isaac felt Reuben breathing down his neck? Have her accusations towards her brother been enough to make him leave without her? She glances again at the pots and clothing flung across the kitchen. Perhaps he had had no choice.

Her throat tightens. She needs to get to the harbour. Needs to look for the lugger. The fishermen at least will know if Isaac has left.

She hurries towards the cliff path.

FRAGILE LIGHT

At the back of a cave beaten into the Polperro cliffs, the light is hatched and fragile. With each exhalation of the sea, the tide grazes the rim of the rock, washing away the footprints that lead down from the edge of the beach.

Caroline kneels with her spine pressed to the back of the cave, one hand full of Mary, the other tight around Gabriel's arm. The light is hatched and fragile, but peer into the cave at the right angle and she knows they will be seen.

They were to have their escape. A thing she and Isaac have been speaking of since the first days of their marriage. Once, escape had been a wild fantasy, whispered of beneath the bedclothes in the same breath as French champagne and voyages around the world. Later, a desperately longed for dream. And finally, since Isaac had found the new buyer in Bodmin, escape had begun to feel tangible.

But their escape was not supposed to be like this.

"Tonight," Isaac had said that morning, sitting on the edge of the bed. Caroline had slept little, still jittery from her clash with Asher Hales. "I'm to go to Bodmin. Make the sale. The moment I get back to the cottage, we leave. We'll have one of the men take us to Fowey from the eastern beach. Find passage out of Cornwall from there."

And Caroline had let herself grip a little tighter to that elusive life of freedom. A life free of Asher and Jacob and all their secrets.

She knelt, her eyes level with her husband's, her knees pressing against his thigh. She wanted to feel his hands in her hair, his lips on hers. Wanted the distance between them to disappear.

It didn't matter, she told herself. It didn't matter that his eyes were lowered and his arms folded stiffly across his chest. Once they had left this place, he would let her in. Once Talland was a memory they would find each other again.

She kissed his cheek. "I'll ready the house as you asked."

When he had left for the fishing port, she dressed hurriedly and pulled the trunk from beneath the bed. She tossed in her few pieces of clothing, along with Isaac's spare shirt and breeches. She went to the kitchen. Emptied the shelves of pots and candles and wiped them free of dust. She took the fish kettle from above the fire and scooped the ash from the grate. Let there be no trace of them left in the cottage. Let there be nothing for Jacob or Asher to find if either of them were to come looking.

The knock at the door was violent, insistent. Two of Reuben's footmen pushed past her into the house.

"Where is your husband?"

And with the footman's fierce words, fear blazed down Caroline's spine. Reuben knew of Isaac's run. There could be no doubt.

She glared at the men, not speaking.

They eyed the bare shelves, the packed trunk. "Planning to leave are you?" One reached into the chest and flung two of the pots across the kitchen. They clattered loudly against the table leg. "Escaping?" He overturned the trunk, kicking the clothes across the floor.

"Get out of my house," hissed Caroline. A fist to her stomach. She doubled over, gasping for breath.

Gabriel rushed from the bedroom in his nightshirt. "Mammik!"

"Get back in your room," Caroline coughed. "Stay with Mary."

One of the men snatched a fistful of her hair, forcing her to look at him. "Where is your husband?"

"He's not here."

They charged into the bedroom, searching. Then they threw open the door to the children's room. Gabriel's fingers were tight around the rim of the cradle, his cheeks wet with tears. Caroline ushered him behind her and stood protectively in front of the crib.

"Tell us where your husband is."

"Where do you think he is? He's at sea. Trying to make a living seeing the bastard you work for has taken everything we have."

And the men were gone.

Caroline bent over the crib, trying to find the breath that had been knocked from her. The muscles in her stomach were throbbing. She threw open the wardrobe and tossed out Gabriel's coat and breeches. She knelt, clutching his shoulders. "Get dressed. Quickly. We need to leave."

They would not beat Reuben's men to Polperro. The thugs would make for the harbour and wait for Isaac to return. Perhaps even sail out to meet him.

But there could be no staying here. Reuben knew of Isaac's plans for certain, and he would want him punished.

Caroline hurried to the bedroom and pulled out the pouch of money Isaac had hidden beneath the mattress. It wasn't enough. Not even close. But somehow they would find a way.

Would Reuben's men be waiting outside the house? Watching her the way they had once watched Isaac and Scarlett try to slip out from beneath Reuben's eyes?

She had to risk it. How to get to Polperro? The cliff path would be quicker, but it would leave them exposed. Take them past Reuben's mansion. Too dangerous. The path through Killigarth was longer, but they would be hidden among houses and trees. They could wind down towards the harbour in the shadow of the hills.

She threw on her cloak and bonnet. In the children's room, Gabriel was lacing his boots, his eyes wide and fearful. She yanked his hair into a tail, pulled him from the floor and knotted a scarf around his neck.

Money. Warm clothes. Mary in blankets, scooped from the cradle. She rushed from the house without looking back.

As she approached the water, Caroline could see the masts of the lugger silhouetted at the edge of the bay. But there, at the other end of the harbour, was Will Francis, roping one of the fishing dories to the moorings. She hurried towards him, hot and breathless. Felt her skin prickling beneath her shift.

Will looked up in surprise. "Mrs Bailey?"

"I have to get to Isaac," she said. "Reuben's men are after him. They know of the run. We need to leave."

His face darkened. He began to unwind the boat's moorings. "I'll go for him."

"Reuben's men will be watching for the lugger," said Caroline.

Will nodded. "I'll bring him back in the dory." He pointed towards the black rock face that slid sharply onto the beach. "In there. There's a cave where we hide the contraband. You see it?"

She nodded.

"Hide in there. You'll not be seen from the land." He glanced at the children; both staring up at him with enormous brown eyes. "You need help getting there?"

"I can manage," said Caroline. "Just fetch my husband. Please."

Isaac doesn't speak as the dory cuts through the swell. He glances over his shoulder at the cave where his family is hiding. Glances at the harbour for any sign of Reuben and his men.

He had heard Will's words only distantly as he had rowed towards the lugger.

Your family.

Reuben.

He knows.

For a moment, the world had lost its colour. Distantly, Isaac heard Will say: "Get in the boat."

And then he was rowing, rowing, tearing oars through the water until his arms burned.

He has no thought of how they will escape this place without tickets on a passenger ship. Walls of cliffs on either side of the village. Reuben will expect them to leave by sea. There will be men watching the harbour. Men watching the roads in and out of town.

Isaac leaps from the boat the moment it bumps against the moorings. And he stops. On the harbour's edge stands the traders' banker, the most loyal of Reuben's men. Their eyes meet.

He cannot go to the cave. Cannot lead the banker to where his family is hiding.

The banker's hand goes to his pocket.

A pistol there, yes. Message received.

Fourteen years ago, Isaac had stood on the beach and had this man hold a gun to his head. The banker had threatened to shoot if he had tried to leave Talland.

Empty threats, Isaac had thought at the time. But with seven-year-old Scarlett clinging to his hand, there had been little room for risk.

He feels his own pistol against his hip.

The banker won't shoot. Not here in the middle of the village. He may be loyal to Reuben, but surely he'll not put his head in a noose for another man's cause.

Follow him to the cave, however, and they will be hidden from the authorities. Isaac will find out just how empty the banker's threats are.

He begins to walk. Step, step, step. Up the hill. Away from the cave, away from his family. Footsteps behind him. Isaac glances over his shoulder. The banker has his pistol out.

"How did he know?" Isaac asks darkly.

"He found the ankers you hid in the tunnel."

"Reuben went to the inn?" What of Flora? Isaac slides his hand into his pocket. Wraps his fingers around the gun.

"Don't," says the banker.

Isaac turns slowly. Wind lashes his hair across his eyes. He brings his hand slowly from his pocket. The banker's shot is frantic, uncontrolled. It flies over Isaac's shoulder and splinters the cold air. Isaac whips out his pistol, hands shaking with the sudden rush of energy. The banker's gun is empty. Isaac could shoot. Run to the cave and find his family. There would be one less man trying to block their escape.

But he thinks of the dizziness that had seized him when he had pulled the trigger on Leach's crewmate. In his mind's eye, he sees the dead man fall. Feels the hot weight of it in his stomach. A line of sweat runs down his back.

"Go," he tells the banker. "Get out of here."

The banker climbs to his feet, eyes not leaving the pistol. Isaac holds out his hand. "Give me your gun."

The banker hands it to him slowly. Begins to walk. When he reaches the top of the hill, he turns. Calls down to Isaac, his words carrying on the wind.

"You go to your family. We'll go for the witch who helped you hide your goods."

LIGHTLESSNESS

Isaac finds them in the cave. Caroline is kneeling in the sand, her back pressed to the wet black rock, an arm tight around each of the children. The sight of them alive and unharmed brings a sound of relief from the back of Isaac's throat. And he is on his knees beside them, feeling the children's soft hair against his cheek. Caroline latches an arm around his neck and pulls him towards her.

"I have the money from beneath the mattress," she says, her voice close to his ear. "We can make it around the point on foot. Get Will to bring the dory to us."

Her plan is a good one. The best they have. Isaac feels a sudden, unexpected swell of love for his wife. The guilt he has been ignoring rears up inside him. A part of him wants nothing more than to take his family and run around that point, into the dory, into the bay. A part of him wants nothing more than to sail away from this life and hope it will lead him back to the woman he married. But there are men heading for the Mariner's Arms to punish Flora for helping him. The thought of her in danger makes sickness rise in his throat. He presses his palms to Caroline's cheeks. "Go," he says. "Take the children around the point. I'll send Will to find you."

"What about you?"

He can't look at her. "Reuben's men are going after Flora. They want to punish her for hiding the ankers. I have to go and help her. I'm sorry."

Caroline's eyes flash. "No," she says. "No, Isaac. We need to leave right now."

"And if Flora and Bess were to be killed because we just ran away and left them?"

Caroline inhales at his sharpness. He feels her eyes boring into him. But she gives a faint nod. "Hurry back," she says huskily. "Please."

Isaac nods. "Go. Take the children."

"No. We're staying here. We'll not leave without you."

Guilt, more guilt. He kisses her forehead. "I'll be back as fast as I can."

Caroline snatches his arm as he turns to leave. "Don't take the cliff path," she says. "There's nowhere to hide."

Isaac nods. Runs from the cave and up the inland path.

From the top of the cliff, Scarlett can see the lugger; a tiny shape in the morning haze. Is Isaac out fishing? Or has he taken his family and left?

She crouches, gulps for breath. Her legs are aching and her lungs burn.

And she sees him.

No. He ought to have been thrown into the hold of a naval ship. Ought to be eating hard tack half way to the Caribbean war.

But no, Asher is here on the clifftop, eyes distant, as though he has come to imagine himself in a place far better than this.

His face is blue and yellow with bruising, his shirt grimy with old, brown blood. The strand of hair hanging loose from his queue is coiled and stiff with sea. He turns away when he sees her charging towards him.

"Was this your doing?" she cries. "Did you go to the revenue men? Is that why my family has left?"

He glances at her wet clothes. "What are you talking about, Scarlett?" His voice is tired. There is a new hunch to his shoulders. A new droop to his chin. The glassiness in his eyes makes her wary. What, she wonders, is a proud man like Asher Hales capable of when his world begins to crumble?

"Did you see my brother's ship leave?" she asks.

He squints. "He left, yes. With the fishing fleet. This morning."

"With the fishing fleet? Did it seem as though he were coming back?"

Asher chuckles. "Here you are wanting my help again."

Scarlett's anger flares. "Tell me what you saw, Asher! I need to know if my family has left."

He stares out at the tiny shape of the lugger. "She is leaving, yes. And taking with her all she knows."

"What? Who are you talking about? Caroline?"

"Yes. Caroline. She is leaving."

"Where is she? Where is Isaac? Have you seen them?"

"She knows," Asher says distantly. "She knows how to find the money."

"What are you talking about? What money? Avery's money?"

He nods.

Scarlett tugs at her hair in frustration. "You're making no sense, Asher. What happened to you?" She knows the answer, of course. Jacob is what had happened. "How did you get away from the press gang?" she asks, her eyes falling to the beads of blood staining the front of his shirt.

Asher snorts. "Through no help of yours."

"What happened to my father?"

"Do you care?"

"No." She narrows her eyes. "You're here to turn us in. That's why you've come back, ayes?"

"They're in the cave," he says suddenly, pointing down to Polperro and the columns of rock on the edge of the beach. "Your family. I saw them."

"My family is in the cave?"

"Yes."

"Why?"

"I don't know." Weariness in his voice. "They're hiding. But you need to go there. Tell her she can't leave."

Scarlett stares at him. Tries to see behind the blank façade of his eyes. She has been foolish enough to trust him before. If she were to walk into that cave she could be easily trapped. Trapped by revenue officers. Trapped by Reuben and his men. Perhaps trapped by Asher himself. She has no idea what he is capable of.

But the cottage has been emptied. It is clear her family will not be returning. What choice does she have but to go to the cave? What choice does she have but to trust?

The light is hatched and fragile. With each exhalation of the sea, the tide grazes the rim of the cave, washing away Isaac's footprints that lead back to the edge of the beach.

Caroline can't shake her anger at his leaving. With rational eyes, she knows he is right to do it. They cannot leave Flora and Bess to face Reuben's men alone. But there is no room for rationality. Only fear and impatience. Anger that burns beneath her skin. She can't help but wonder where Isaac's loyalties lie.

She tries to slow her breathing. The children can sense her fear, she is sure. Mary is wriggling in her arms, mewling, grappling at the hem of her cloak. Gabriel is a barrage of questions.

What are we doing?
What's happening?
Where is Tasik going?

A sudden change in the rhythm of the water, as though legs are moving through the shallows. Caroline holds her breath. Pins hard eyes on Gabriel to silence him.

Is someone there?

Instinct tells her to run; leave this cave, this village, this land where her secrets hang so thick in the air. What had she been thinking, building a life here, upon the ghosts of her most regretful of deeds? Jacob is right. She had been a fool to stay.

The noise comes again. Legs sighing through the water. This time there can be no doubt.

It could be any of them, Caroline realises. Asher coming for money. Jacob and Reuben for retribution. Tom Leach hunting and seeking the voice who had turned him in.

Gabriel knots his fingers in her skirts. In the light spilling through the narrow opening, she sees his eyes are wide and fearful.

Mary whines against her shoulder. Caroline smooths her hair, rubs her cheek, her back.

Quiet now. Quiet.

A shadow passes over the mouth of the cave.

One way in. One way out.

Caroline looks over her shoulder. Beside her, the chasm extends into a narrow, lightless passage. She cannot hope to fit inside it. But her children will. She hands Mary to Gabriel. "Take her," she whispers. "Get as far back as you can."

Gabriel murmurs in fear. "What about you?"

She kisses his cheek. "Go on. Hurry. Be brave."

He nods wordlessly and wriggles into the passage. Mary stares back over his shoulder, her face crumpled and tearful. Caroline stares into her daughter's eyes until they vanish into the dark.

THE DROWNED MAN'S CAVE

The cave is close. Scarlett tries to peer into it from the edge of the beach. She sees nothing but rock and dark.

How many times had she sat on this beach as a child, telling stories with Bobby Carter of the drowned smuggler haunting the cave?

"Step inside," he had dared her. "Are you scared?"

Her stomach knots as she edges towards the slit in the rock. She longs for ghost stories. Tales of drowned sailors. Longs for the ethereal and intangible.

There is a shape inside the cave. A figure, lying on the sand.

Caroline.

Scarlett hurries inside and drops to her knees. She reaches fingers towards Caroline's neck. Her pulse is fast. Alive. A line of blood runs down the side of her head. Scarlett gives her shoulder a gentle shake. Caroline stirs. Her eyelids flutter.

A murmur in the darkness. Scarlett turns abruptly. Gabriel is crouching in the narrow passage at the back of the cave, eyes swollen with tears. His arms are tight around his sister. Scarlett hurries towards them, pulls Gabriel into her arms. Can he feel her heart thumping against her ribs? He mumbles in fear against her wet shoulder. Scarlett plants a kiss in his hair.

"Did you see who did this?" she whispers. "Is someone here?" The cave is small. There is no one else in here with them. But the rest of the cliff is rugged and sliced with hiding places. Is whoever attacked Caroline still hiding in the dark?

Gabriel shakes his head against her chest. "Mammik told me to hide." His fingers dig into her neck. She hears herself whisper calming words she doesn't believe.

It's all right.

Don't be afraid.

She feels Gabriel stiffen. He pulls free from her arms and points a shaking finger into the blackness.

A noise from behind her. Movement on the edge of her vision. A half-swallowed cry from Gabriel. For a fleeting moment, she feels the air around her move.

And then there is pain.

And then there is black.

The Mariner's Arms is quiet. The street is quiet. Isaac hears the wings of a bird beat above his head. It feels as though the village is holding its breath, waiting to Reuben to strike.

He knocks. His heart is drumming. He had taken the inland path as Caroline had asked; a longer journey than the exposed ribbon over the cliffs. What if he is too late?

He sighs in relief when Flora pulls open the door.

"You're still here," she says. "You need to leave. Reuben, he found—"

"Get Bessie," Isaac tells her, "and come with me. Quickly."

She stays planted in the doorway, the green globe of the watch ball circling, circling above her head. "Did Scarlett find you?"

"What?"

"She was here when Reuben found the ankers. She went to your cottage to warn you."

Isaac exhales sharply. "We'll find her." He tugs Flora's hand. "You can't stay here." He tells her of the smugglers' banker and the threats he had made. Tells her of the way he had disappeared over the cliffs towards the inn. And he sees that infuriating hardness fall over Flora's eyes. That infuriatingly admirable stubbornness he has come to know so well.

She pulls her hand free. "I'm not leaving. I'll not be scared from my home."

"What about Bessie?" Isaac gestures wildly at the watch ball. "You mean to protect her with this? Magic is not going to save you, Flora. You used to know that. It won't save you from Reuben and it won't save you from Leach."

Her jaw tightens. He expects an eruption, but she grips his shoulders to still him. "No one is here, Isaac. No one is coming for me. Whatever the banker told you was a lie."

He stands motionless for a moment. Has he been a fool to leave his family in the cave? Has he fallen for empty threats, so Reuben might put a stop to their escape? His hike back to Talland will have given Reuben time to block the roads out of Polperro. Given him time to station men at the mouth of the harbour. Isaac sucks in his breath. "Christ. I need to leave."

"Yes," says Flora, her eyes on his. "You must."

And so this is the end, he realises. The end of sneaking down the tunnel to see her, the end of fire and brandy and hot stones beneath them, the end of this thing that had left him lit up inside the way he hadn't been for years.

For the best. He can't hope to fix things with Caroline while he is drawn to the light from the inn on the hill.

He can't say it. Can't handle the finality of *goodbye*. So he takes her face in his hands and pushes his lips hard against hers.

Flora pulls away abruptly at the sound of footsteps behind them. "Caroline—" She starts to say, but she is silenced by the coldness in his wife's eyes.

Isaac watches a look of wild anger pass across Caroline's face, but it is replaced quickly by a different horror. She looks past Flora, her eyes meeting Isaac's in desperation. Her words are a garble, beads of dried blood clinging to her cheek.

Scarlett, she says. And *men.* And then she speaks with sudden, sickening clarity.

"The children. They've been taken."